PROGENY OF THE ADDER

Leslie H. Whitten was born in Jacksonville, Florida in 1928. He was an investigative reporter in Washington D.C. (covering, among other things, the Watergate scandal), a poet, a translator of Baudelaire, and the author of nearly a dozen novels, including several in the horror genre: *Progeny of the Adder* (1965), *Moon of the Wolf* (1967), *The Alchemist* (1973), and *The Fangs of Morning* (1994). He died at age 89 in 2017.

Cover: The cover reproduces the cover painting (uncredited) from the 1975 Avon paperback edition.

D1594023

PROGENY
OF THE
ADDER

LESLIE H. WHITTEN
INTRODUCTION BY
WILL ERRICKSON

VALANCOURT BOOKS

Dedication: To P. W.

Progeny of the Adder by Leslie H. Whitten
Originally published by Doubleday in 1965

Copyright © 1965 by Leslie H. Whitten
Republished by arrangement with the Estate of Leslie H. Whitten
Introduction copyright © 2022 by Will Errickson

"Paperbacks from Hell" logo designed by Timothy O'Donnell.
© 2017 Quirk Books. Used under license. All rights reserved.

Cover art taken from the 1975 Avon paperback edition. Despite
extensive searches and inquiries, no record of copyright
registration for the art could be located, nor could the artist be
identified. Anyone with information is invited to contact the
Publisher.

Published by Valancourt Books, Richmond, Virginia
http://www.valancourtbooks.com

ISBN 978-1-954321-60-1 (*paperback*)
Also available as an electronic book.

Cover restoration and design by M. S. Corley
Set in Dante MT

INTRODUCTION

My first encounter with *Progeny of the Adder* came in early 2010 at a bookstore in North Carolina, not long after I began my book blog, Too Much Horror Fiction. I had neither heard of nor seen it before, and I eagerly snatched it up for just a couple of dollars. With its red-tinged vampire cover art and bearing the distinctive, red-dyed page edges so common on old mass-market paperbacks (which publishers used for brand identification), *Progeny* felt like a secret discovery, precisely the kind of obscure horror novel I wanted to feature on my new blog. As I read *Progeny*, I was reminded of several other vintage works of vampire entertainment and would soon learn of the novel's unheralded place in horror history. Nothing like being late to the party! But can we say, now with this lovely new edition from Valancourt Books, that I was at least *fashionably* late?

In 1970, a struggling actor and writer named Jeff Rice wrote a novel he called *The Kolchak Papers*, about a cranky detective chasing an honest-to-God, real-life vampire around Las Vegas. Before it was even published it was bought by television producers, and, with a teleplay written by Richard *"I Am Legend"* Matheson, turned into the hugely popular 1972 TV-movie *The Night Stalker*. Rice's novel only came out as a tie-in edition, now titled, of course, *The Night Stalker*, by Pocket Books and with Matheson's name prominently printed on the cover.

Around the same time, the two low-budget but eerily effective *Count Yorga* movies would also place a decidedly vintage-style vampire (Robert Quarry, thank you very much) in the modern world. The publication of Stephen King's own autumnal account of vampires feasting on contemporary Americans, *'Salem's Lot*, was only a few short years away. Christopher Lee's unstoppable Count went *Dracula A.D.* in 1972; undead African Prince Mamuwalde stalked the streets and funk clubs of Los Angeles' Black neighborhoods in *Blacula*. Ultimately this conceit, like all good ideas, would become a joke: caped, tuxedoed, and tanned George Hamilton and his potential snack, liberated woman Susan St. James, dancing to the disco hit "I Love the Nightlife" in the 1979 comedy *Love at First Bite*.

As you can see, when this new decade dawned, vampires were crawling from their crypts not in candlelit, cobwebbed castles, but here, today, escaping from their shadowy Gothic and folkloric origins into the wild 'n' woolly Seventies—and beyond. Their victims weren't bosomy barmaids or village virgins, but cosmopolitan women who smelled of Charlie by Revlon, smoked Virginia Slims, and sported Jackie O sunglasses. Rising crime, inflation, political corruption, the Vietnam War, smog . . . and now vampires: what a time to be alive!

But author and journalist Leslie H. Whitten (1928-2017) was there first. Published in 1965, *Progeny of the Adder*, his first novel, was set in Washington, D.C., in the early Sixties. It features a beleaguered young homicide detective on the trail of a killer who's dumping the blood-drained bodies of prostitutes into the Potomac. Without doubt it is the wellspring from which all those old-school creatures of the night slithered into our contemporary world of high-rise apartments and rundown tenements, used-car salesmen and nightly television newscasts. "As a boy," Whitten is on record stating, "I got interested in the original *Dracula*. One Saturday when my wife and I were fighting, I went down to the Library of Congress and began to read more about vampires. It was cheaper than my psychoanalysis and almost as good. In my books I've taken a lot of the ancient lore and put it in a modern setting." His son, also named Les, recalls how his father was "fascinated" by vampires. "I have very early memories of my brothers and I watching the Bela Lugosi *Dracula* with him," Les says today. "We talked about it all the time."

How *Progeny* came to be published is a writer's dream: around 1963 or '64, Whitten entered his first novel in a contest held by publisher Doubleday for "best amateur writer." Even though he came in second place, Doubleday released it—in hardcover, no less, via their Crime Club imprint. Its dust jacket bore an ominous steamer trunk. Ace released it in paperback in 1968, with a gothic romance-style cover of a woman menaced by a black cloak-clad, hirsute, vampire-looking dude with giant clawed hands. And then in 1975 came the Avon paperback, bearing the cover art on this reprint edition, artist unknown, alas. The last time *Progeny* was in print was 1992, when Leisure Books stuck it together with another Whitten book, *Moon of the Wolf*, in a cheapie twofer paperback (*A $9.00 Value for Only $4.99!*).

Leslie Hunter Whitten, Jr.'s biography is a unique one for a horror writer: born in Florida and raised in the nation's capital, he joined the Army after quitting college. Whitten then moved to Paris as a young man to become a poet. That didn't quite work out, so he returned to the States to continue schooling. Later he became a well-known, highly respected journalist whose investigative career included fearless writing about Watergate and the mob, becoming an enemy of Nixon and trailed by the CIA. He was even arrested once by the FBI. Whitten wrote novels throughout the late Sixties and Seventies and was eventually successful enough to do it full time. His obituary in *The New York Times* was headlined "muckraking journalist"—it does not mention *Progeny* at all—and elsewhere Whitten referred to himself as a "swashbuckler." *Progeny* sold well enough that Whitten wrote three more books in the genre: the aforementioned *Moon of the Wolf* (1967), set in Mississippi and made into a TV-movie in 1972, *The Alchemist* (1973), an occult thriller taking place in D.C., and later, *The Fangs of Morning* (1994). In 1981, Stephen King himself deemed it "a particularly important work" in his classic horror study *Danse Macabre*, but *Progeny* would, because of *The Night Stalker* television phenomenon, be forgotten by all but the most rabid vampire fans.

Progeny of the Adder is, at heart, a police procedural. We follow youngish Washington, D.C. Homicide Detective Harry Picard step by painstaking step as he delves into a distressing, disturbing case of murdered prostitutes—"whores," in the unfortunate vulgar term of the era. The women are underweight, their throats gashed open and their corpses found in the Potomac River, which borders Maryland and Washington D.C. Whitten details Harry's every move in plain and clear and precise prose, placing you right in the thick of the case. It's not always action-packed; there is more paperwork and legwork in police detection than gunplay and strong-arming.

Forensic details, grim from the first, are more graphic than television and more serious than horror movies of the day: *"The woman's blond hair was partially pushed out of her face . . . her lips were pale and the great bloodless gash that he knew had killed her stood out on her throat like a colored drawing in a medical book. This is death, the thought struck him, color me red."*

Whitten was familiar with cops and their beats, his son Les says, and hung around police stations and knew their operating procedures. You can feel that familiarity in the pages, in hieroglyphics like "UNKNOWN, fem. March 23, picard-hom., #132-63", in the politicking that must be done between superiors, inferiors, witnesses, lowlifes, tabloid newspeople, in the nitty-gritty of gathering and sifting through evidence such as clothing labels, used tissues, partial license plates, forged signatures. Whitten gets at the conflict between the police and the politicians, especially after one of the victims is discovered to be the daughter of a prominent dignitary official visiting D.C.

The supernatural aspect is in doubt throughout: maybe the deranged killer only *thinks* he is a vampire? Identified as Sebastien Paulier, according to witness statements he is a black-clad, detestable-smelling, and powerfully strong "foreigner" slathered in fake suntan cream. With no luck catching Paulier, policewoman Suzanne Finnerton, a divorced Austrian émigré—and Picard's love interest—is tapped to go undercover as a streetwalker to tempt the killer from his lair. The city is in a panic; the news reports mention "vampirism," hemoythmia, delusion. Picard reads a detailed foreign report on Paulier's whereabouts before his arrival in D.C.: he had run a plantation in the Malay Peninsula and was referred to by his terrified workers—nay, slaves— as being like a *penanggalan* (wait till you learn about *that* vampiric creature). And as is *de rigueur* for searchers after horror, Picard heads to the Library of Congress to research vampire lore; you'll get a crash course in all things loathsome and bloodsucking.

I envy readers who are going to experience for the first time the confrontations between Picard and Paulier, in which Whitten delivers with real suspense the kind of boredom and terror that accompanies police work. Scenes set in an old farmhouse and an abandoned apartment building crackle with suspense, dread, and despair. The grim quotidian reality of those set pieces, put down in Whitten's stark pen, no doubt presages King's own vampire hunters confronting Kurt Barlow at the climax of *'Salem's Lot*. But Les Whitten was there first.

As for the book's elusive title, at first I thought it might be an obscure biblical reference, or perhaps something from Shakespeare; helpfully Whitten made it the book's epigraph. I was quite surprised to find it a line from one of my favorite poets, Charles Baudelaire, part of his 1857 poem "Burial": "The spider will spin her fatal net / The adder spawn her progeny."

For those of you not up on your 19th-century French decadent/symbolist poets, Baudelaire (1821-1867) originated the quote *"La plus belle des ruses du diable est de vous persuader qu'il n'existe pas,"* which everyone now knows from the 1995 crime movie *The Usual Suspects*: "The greatest trick the devil ever pulled is convincing the world he doesn't exist." Baudelaire isn't just some poet guy; he is widely considered the greatest of all French poets and is of some interest to horror fans: his excellent translations of Edgar Allan Poe made that American writer famous in Europe, which in turn solidified Poe's reputation in the States.

Baudelaire also wrote some beautifully grotesque poetry that would make any goth or gorehound weep with unhallowed joy (I'm thinking in particular of "A Carcass," from his infamous *Flowers of Evil,* in which two lovers on a romantic walk discover a rotting corpse in the brush). In his free time Whitten translated many Baudelaire writings into English, and in the 2000s published them. If you can't tell, I absolutely adore the fact that the title of a groundbreaking pulp vampire novel derives from such a pedigree.

Unfortunately, *The Night Stalker* has overshadowed *Progeny* for decades, primarily because popular culture tells us that a book isn't really anything until it is made into a movie (also: Darren McGavin made a pretty great character in Kolchak). But it's undeniable: the prosaic protagonist in a realistically described modern city on the hunt for an unbeknownst-to-him supernatural force was really locked into place well before Jeff Rice wrote his own book. Richard Matheson said the similarities between the two stories was "sheer coincidence," Joe R. Lansdale says *Progeny* was "undoubtedly the influence," while Whitten and his publisher felt those similarities, and more, were evidence of plagiarism. But Jeff Rice denied ever reading Whitten's book. The whole matter was dropped.

Whitten's son Les is less forgiving about Rice: "He got away with it," he says now, while noting his father knew the matter couldn't be proved legally. Many articles and blogs and message boards have chewed on this topic for years now, but what really matters is this: *Progeny of the Adder* is back in print, readily available now for horror fans to see how Les Whitten originated one of modern horror's most enduring myths—the vampire no longer representing Old World fears and superstitions, but now a part of our contemporary psyche, stalking modern streets and still, as ever, finding prey ripe for the taking.

WILL ERRICKSON
April 14, 2022

WILL ERRICKSON is a lifelong horror enthusiast and author of the *Too Much Horror Fiction* blog, where he rediscovers forgotten titles and writers and celebrates the genre's resplendent cover art. With Grady Hendrix in 2017, he co-wrote the Bram Stoker Award-winning *Paperbacks from Hell*, which featured many books from his personal collection. Today Will resides in Portland, Oregon, with his wife Ashley and his ever-growing library of vintage horror paperbacks.

If on a night that's close and hot
Some Christian, out of decency,
Down where the tombstones crack and rot
Buries your corpse, your vanity

There where the stars have chastely set
Shutting their eyelids leadenly
The spider will spin her fatal net,
The adder spawn her progeny.

—Baudelaire
Translated by L. H. W.

Homicide detective Harry Picard stood on the muddy bank at Fletcher's Cove and stared at the Potomac. The river, now that spring had melted the upstream snow, was high. The tops of the small trees and underbrush made eddies near the bank.

It was a tough, ugly river at this time of the year: fast-moving, with no time for the nonsense of fishing or boating or for love-making on its banks.

Two days ago this river had swept into this same bank the body of a young woman, but one that only the old coroner, Doc Kip, could identify as young. The river and its scavenging fish had done their work. Flesh was gone from the face, the hands, almost every place not covered by the mud-weighted clothes.

Ugly, of course. But it seemed a routine river death. Picard watched a heavy log in the river trundled downstream toward Washington city by the channel current. He reviewed the two days since the body was washed in to shore and snagged on the submerged underbrush.

A young morgue attendant, his head twisted away as he loaded the rubberized "sleeping bag" containing the body into the wagon, had said, "Harry, she was down all winter and she has to pick the week I'm on days to come up."

At the morgue later that day the Identification Bureau's senior technician had inspected what was left of the woman's hands.

No chance, he had told Picard, who had hoped that one finger pad might be complete enough so that glycerine could be injected beneath the skin to firm it for a print, or that permanganate could be used to harden a portion of the whorls.

"We can try to get you some identification on the teeth, Harry," the technician had said. "And you can maybe make out something on the clothes. But that's all we can do on this one."

Picard, accustomed to working with no more than that, had quickly obtained the coroner's permission for preserving the skull and its unique array of filled and unfilled teeth.

Doc Kip, as pallid as his charges, had been coroner for forty years and each year he threatened to retire. Lately, he worked only a half day. The rest of the time he indulged what he loved most. Its simple symbolism made it an often-repeated city story. He loved most to deliver babies.

Detective Sergeant Picard had questioned him about the body.

"Nothing to tell, nothing except negative things," the old doctor replied. "No bones broken, no slugs. The arms and legs and face are too gone to tell about wounds, Harry.

"She lost some blood somewhere in the couple of months she was in the river, or before she got in. No pathology, tumors, far as I can see."

Picard grunted dismally, remembering the condition of her face and hands. He lit a cigarette, dragging deeply on it. Death like this was uncommonly ugly.

"Sorry, m'boy," said Doc Kip, and shuffled toward his office.

In another room Picard found two attendants laying out the sodden clothes. He lifted the three-quarter-length coat, once a decent wool garment, and smoothed its label with his thumb: a mass-sale downtown store. The dress, flattened and oozing brackish water onto a formica table, was low-cut, maybe a little too low-cut, and had only a manufacturer's label.

Picard liked to do things while he had them fresh in

his mind. The Police Department had a policewoman attached to the Women's Bureau who specialized in tracing clothes and identification of fabrics. She could be helpful, Picard had mused, and moreover she was an intriguing woman—a short, trim blonde with an unexpected Austrian accent. Her name was Suzanne Finnerton.

An émigrée, she had married a police lieutenant and divorced him five years later when alcohol and a precinct captaincy proved too much for him; he left the force, the city, and recently the land of the living. As part of the clannish police world, she had few contacts, and when he left she gratefully took the job offered her by the protective Department as their clothing expert.

Picard rang her extension, looking forward to the banter that was the outside limit of her relationship with the detectives. She was out. He left a note asking her to read his homicide report and then see if she could discover any clue to the dead woman's identity from the clothing.

The next day—yesterday—she had called him and delivered her findings crisply.

No, nothing very much she could determine, she said with a light roll of the r's. The woman wore a Size 12. The dress was made in Manhattan and was distributed from Bangor to Miami. The store that sold the coat of course had no recollection of it other than that they had stocked it two or three years ago. Yes, they would check receipts. The style of the dress. Well, it was a somewhat gaudy silk-crepe, the sort a housewife with slightly flashy taste would have as her second-best dress, or a waitress's best, or a young prostitute. Yes, a woman twenty-two or twenty-three—Doc Kip's estimate of her age—would buy that kind of dress.

"Thanks for your trouble, Susy," Picard said.

"You are most welcome, my good Sergeant Picard," she said with just a trace of flippancy.

Picard, turning from the Potomac, could see nothing he had omitted during those last two days. He was a worrier, one who would call into the Homicide Bureau after he got home to have a colleague read him the names on the report he had just made. He would compare them with his notebook. He was not ashamed of this trait, because the worrying opened up trains of thought that sometimes led to something forgotten. But this time he could think of nothing.

The detective slogged upstream through the mud toward Chain Bridge, running what he knew of the case through his mind. His shoes clotted with mud and he grumbled to himself:

"I ought to wear rubbers. I ought to get me a wife that would make me wear the damned things." He was thirty-three.

He looked up at the bridge. Its sturdy, unlovely vaults made a broad concrete scar on the green land and blue sky.

Women don't go walking in low-cut dresses in the winter on the muddy banks of a river, Picard thought. They don't go boating in that kind of clothes. If they want to walk they wear slacks and if they want to make love they stay in cars.

He squinted at the bridge again. I would bet on the bridge, he thought. If she walked down to the bank through the woods, she'd have been somebody from around here who'd know how, and there's no missing-person report on anybody like her. And if somebody wanted to get rid of her, he'd have been a damned fool to drag her through muddy woods, leaving tracks and risking that she wouldn't stay down in the shallow water by the banks.

Suicide? No. The downtown bridges, Key and Taft and Calvert, were the ones that attracted the suicides. They were just a walk or a quick taxi from the bars, the hotel rooms, and the apartments where people made up their minds to do away with themselves.

Why would anyone, particularly if the girl were a prostitute from downtown or a city lush, come miles upriver to jump? He jotted himself a note to get a paragraph in the taxi circulars asking for information on fares to the area of the bridge—"distraught woman, 22–25, dressed . . ." It was something to be done as part of the routine.

Accidental? What hapless drunk would walk in the woods in a party dress, or across a bridge far from the nearest town? Who falls in rivers in winter by accident?

Many questions, he mused, but no answers.

Picard was ready to turn back. He picked up a stick and began to push the black river mud from his shoe sides.

Thrown off the bridge? Maybe so. Or a nut: a nut could have done anything with herself. The river was in Washington's jurisdiction up to the Virginia shore. That made it a Washington case, his case now.

The detective cut back to the road through the woods. He still carried the stick. He poked a little hole in the ground half consciously beside the fragile snowdrops and wood violets, as if he wanted to provide evidence that he had duly noted them.

Back in his cruiser, he drove toward headquarters and twenty minutes later was picking his way through downtown traffic when he heard a call come in for him—"Cruiser Twenty-two."

The mechanical sound of the dispatcher's voice continued: "Proceed to Fletcher's Cove, Cruiser Twenty-two." Picard, exasperated, radioed that he had just left the cove.

But the voice was impersonal, imperturbable: "Please return. Another subject has been found in the river. Cruiser Twenty-one will meet you there." That would be the homicide captain, Pulanske.

Picard made a U-turn. Annoyed, he drove rapidly in the direction he had come.

A second "subject" in the river, he thought. It might be just the springtime river yielding those bodies kept down by winter's refrigeration. The gases generated by warmer weather buoyed the corpses to the surface. A second body might be just coincidence, an easy case complete with identification and house key and a suspicion-free suicide note at home. But here were two bodies swirled into the same cove in three days. Instinctively Picard felt there would be no pat answer.

At Fletcher's Cove again, two uniformed policemen and a group of men in overcoats or the surplus field jackets the riverside fishers wore stood in a semicircle where the rough dock of Fletcher's boathouse met the muddy shoreline. Picard shouldered through twenty-five or so men and signaled the two uniformed men to move the onlookers back.

The body was tied to the rear of a rowboat with frayed anchor rope and was face down in the shallow, roily shore water. The first sight of death unnerved him slightly, as it always did, and he lit a cigarette for solace. The tangle of muddy blond hair showed the body to be a woman. Her left hand trailed on the water's surface, the fingers rippled nervously, extended by the current.

There would be enough on this one for a print, Picard speculated with distasteful satisfaction.

Two gawky high-school boys, skipping school for smokes and a hike along the river, had found the body, snagged near shore on a submerged treetop.

They had cut loose one of Fletcher's boats lashed inland and dragged it to the water. The older one had poled out with a broken oar while the other one steadied the boat from shore with anchor ropes tied together.

Picard was amused and pleased at their sense of self-protection. But by the time he got them firmly on the subject of their discovery, first Pulanske, then two reporters and a press photographer, then a police photographer and two more uniformed men arrived. It was the usual mess, with the curious now mingling with the police—and the reporters underfoot.

The detective sergeant briefed his boss deliberately, then walked to the muddy road leading from the street to meet the morgue men.

Pulanske was bucking for inspector, had some friends on Capitol Hill, and never missed a chance to get his name in the paper. But the result of his obliging the reporters in time for the afternoon papers—and without listening to Picard's details—was confusion. The story came out with both boys in the boat.

The morgue attendants promised to take the body directly to the morgue. They picked their way through the newly churned mud to deliver it from the now large group of men.

The Women's Bureau cruiser pulled up behind the morgue wagon, and Picard felt a lift in spirits when he saw the blond head of Susy Finnerton through the windshield bent forward as she took the key from the ignition.

Holding up her nicely cut coat slightly to keep it from mud splatters, she stepped carefully around the mudholes, approaching Picard and looking at him with frank and curious blue eyes.

"What's happening?" she asked, glancing down at the group clustered around Pulanske and the rowboat. A camera flash went off. Pulanske was posed pointing out into the river.

"Big deal, big dealer," she said, her colloquialism sounding peculiar but fetching through her trace of an accent. "Anything to be done down there, Harry?"

"Nope. Another woman. I don't want to go through

her coat pockets until we get her the hell out of the circus." He shook his head toward the river. "Can you go over the clothes?" Then he added with friendly sarcasm, "You came up with so many good answers on the last one."

She made a little mock grimace.

"I'll meet you at the morgue," she said.

"No," he said. "I'll take you."

She started to argue, then changed her mind and told the uniformed woman in her cruiser to notify headquarters of her destination.

"So what do you think?" she inquired as they drove, adding in the same breath, "God, you're muddy."

"Don't know," he said, smiling at her observation. "It would be nice if it was just a coincidence."

Slowly, perhaps under the influence of the clear blue March day, their talk strayed from the case to the more relaxed gossip of the force. Who would be the next chief? When would they retire the deputy? He was dotty three quarters of the time. Pulanske? Yes, they both thought he was a good detective, but he was politicking too much for the promotion. No, he was not a pleasant man to work with. His suspicions about people in general carried over to his subordinates.

"Anything below lieutenant isn't really people to him," Picard sighed.

"Detectives aren't people," she observed. Picard caught a hint of tightness and wondered if she was thinking of her husband.

He ignored her comment. A few minutes later he pulled up at the morgue building. "You want to eat somewhere after this?" He tried to sound offhand.

"Nice place for an invitation," she laughed. "No, thanks, I want to do my duties by you and get back to the bureau."

"How about a martini after work," he said, aware that he was pushing.

"Thanks. No, thanks." They walked toward the building. "What I mean," she said, sensing he was hurt, "what I mean is that I really don't want to make any precedents, not with anybody."

Doc Kip was in a reminiscent mood as they waited for the body to arrive.

"Now here we sit, a contented bunch," he began. They were in his office, sunk into the old leather chairs that smelled so of pipe smoke they masked the characteristic odor of his trade.

"You take a coroner, or a detective, or a newspaperman, somebody that deals all the time with the morbid aspects of living. He's likelier to be satisfied with his lot than the clerk that only sees a body at a funeral, and then all dressed up.

"Dressed up fit to kill," he finished. He looked up with a wry smile at his bad joke and the other two looked at him with mock exasperation. He was garrulous only among those he knew would forgive him.

"Maybe for us there is something healthy in the contrast of seeing death all the time and our own selves being alive. Makes it all a little sweeter, somehow," he said. "Gets some of 'em, though," he added, and Picard knew that they were in for a session of Doc's stories. He was beginning a tale about morgue aides who had released the body of a middle-aged prostitute to a funeral home in place of a dead society woman, when he heard the morgue wagon pull up.

"End of story time," he said, smiling.

Doc Kip worked at the autopsy nimbly and with marvelous efficiency. Susy was inspecting the clothes in the next room. Picard smoked and watched the quick incisions and short delicate strokes of the scalpel.

"How old?" he asked, when the coroner paused.

"Oh, twenty-five, maybe twenty-seven, eight at a stretch."

23

The dead woman's throat had been all but destroyed by the catfish and eels. Her eyes were gone too. Aside from that there was no evidence of wounds.

The detective walked to the window. He could take death in its ugliest forms only in short spells.

"So, what do we have?" he asked Doc Kip.

"Oh," said the coroner, "probably a deep gash on the throat killed her, there where the fish seized at her, and she was in the water say a week, ten days, maybe. She bled to death, or she lost a lot of blood, anyway, a lot of blood."

Dead when she hit the water? Well, probably; there wasn't much water in the lungs. Not like she had hit it alive and breathed it in. Yes, he agreed, the gash and this could mean she was murdered and thrown in the river.

No, nothing under the nails but mud. Yes, he would get that in a specimen envelope for the FBI lab. Nothing in the teeth except a cavity or two. Nope, no bruises, unless there were at the throat—hard to say, there. Oh yes, you'll get prints from this one. Nothing pathological. Well, not really pathological, except she looked like her weight had gone down fast, the way her skin hangs on her.

Doc Kip stopped his running diagnosis a moment and looked up at Picard, and the detective was surprised to see how very sharp the old man's deep brown eyes could be behind the glasses.

"What you want to know is this, Harry. This woman didn't eat anything for a long time before she died—No, don't interrupt me. It's not just that there's nothing in the tummy and the guts—a coupla, three days could do that—it's the way the stomach is constricted, contracted."

"Why?" Picard said, feeling uneasy at the coroner's tone and what he had been told. "Some kind of starvation diet?"

"Now, I don't know that," said Doc Kip softly, relaxed again.

Picard asked if Doc Kip planned to take tissue, to run a

full autopsy, a gentle way of asking him to forego his usual half day off.

"I can, I can," was the absorbed reply.

The detective walked from the room and down the hall, puzzling over the woman's lack of food. He opened the door to the "freezer," a windowless refrigerated room with aluminum drawers for the bodies.

There were two small drawers for infants and one very large one for the obese and for bodies taken from the river in summer. When he was twenty-two, he recalled, and just on the force as a uniformed man, he had played the big shot and stayed for the autopsy on a river case. When the ballooned corpse had been opened, it gave up the gas that had built up in it within the warm river and Picard had run to vomit.

But he was not there today for recollections. He opened the drawer marked "UNKNOWN, fem., March 23, picard-hom., #132-63," and with a few quick tugs he pulled a dozen hairs from the first dead woman's head. He wanted to get them to the FBI for a color and perhaps blood and health analysis. It was the one thing he could remember having forgotten. As he left the room, he smiled inwardly. It was Susy's blond hair that had reminded him to take the samples.

Picard joined her in the room with the most recent victim's clothes. She was taking notes and was all professional.

"Coat from downtown, dress too," said Susy, lifting up the two garments from the broad wooden table. "Dark stockings, bikini pants, sexy bra, half slip," she continued, letting these garments remain on the table. "All of it pretty fair stuff, nothing special."

"Prostitute?" said Harry.

"Well, it could be very well, it's gaudy enough," she said, letting her breath out.

"Housewife?" he asked.

She looked at him in annoyance, not sure whether he was serious. "She didn't have a ring, you know."

"See anything else?" he inquired.

"Well, not really . . . well, maybe yes. When they took these things off I thought she looked a little thin—"

"She was losing weight, Doc Kip noticed," he interrupted, pulled up sharply by Susy's discovery.

"Her dress is a thirteen. It must have been funny, a little baggy on her, you couldn't tell really, the water and all . . ."

"So her clothes were too big," Picard conceded, curious now with the skepticism that made him a good detective. "Let's say for argument's sake she was on some kind of starvation diet."

"So maybe the clothes, the coat, could be explained that way," Susy answered. "But not the bra. She was dressed for a man and the dress is a nice dress, a bit sleazy, but not a five-dollar or ten-dollar prostitute's who wouldn't care how she looked . . . and the dress, too, it's the sort of thing that she wouldn't want too big, even if she was losing weight, she'd take it in, want it probably a little snug. . . . So you see," she went on, talking rapidly but finding things, "these clothes belonged on a good-sized woman, high-waisted and busted. That woman in there is thin, too thin. Particularly she wouldn't wear a brassiere that big."

They threw the idea back and forth.

The woman, then, may have been wearing someone else's clothes. But again not somebody else's bra, and would she borrow a sleazy dress too big? Maybe an ordinary dress, but a party dress? Particularly if she were hustling, she'd want a party dress to fit.

"Some party," said Picard.

The mystery of the weight loss dogged his mind. How could she have lost so much weight so fast? From a wasting disease? The complete autopsy might show this, but Doc

Kip had found nothing pathological so far. Well, couldn't someone have killed her and put somebody else's clothes on her or clothes that were hers in her heavier days?

"Or maybe she was just some kind of nut that liked roomy clothes," said Susy, mocking him. "When you people in homicide don't know, you always say, 'Maybe she was just some kind of nut.'"

Again she begged off a late lunch date with him and he dropped her by the Women's Bureau. Despite the rejection, being with her had somehow made him feel good about himself.

Picard drove through the three-story slums on the way to police headquarters. He no longer saw the hostile stares of the children who played and the adults who loitered along the route. Although his cruiser was unmarked, these people had become leery of every black standard-model car with a radio.

At first he had listened to and even believed the community relations lectures he had been given as a rookie at the police academy. But after the first two attacks on him by street thugs and the first blank stares from people he knew were hiding a suspect, he had grown sophisticated. Now he simply did his job as fairly as he could.

At headquarters he wheeled the cruiser into the detectives' parking lot and walked up the flight of steps leading toward its columned entrance. Motorcycle men in shiny boots, the spit-and-polish men of the First Precinct, spivs, respectable citizens coming to pay tickets, informers, bondsmen, lawyers soliciting business—all came and went in the big building.

Picard thought of a quatrain hung in a judge's anteroom across the square in the courthouse, lines he had memorized while he waited for trials to begin:

★

This is that theater the muse loves best.
All dramas ever dreamed are acted here
Hero and dupe and villain all appear
The roles are done in earnest, none in jest . . .

For him the lines applied even more to police head-quarters, where the dramas were firsthand, the players still hot and steaming from their crime, not secondhand, rehearsed by their attorneys.

Picard walked into the building, bought two ham sandwiches and a pint of milk at the snack bar, and went upstairs to write up his report.

By late afternoon the second woman's prints were in the hands of the FBI and the Identification Bureau. Missing Persons already had assured him that they had no such woman on the open-case list.

There was an indication that she was dressed after the bleeding had stopped, that is, after she was dead. The Identification Bureau based this on the absence of blood on her clothing. They did not think the river could have dissolved every trace of it, even in a week.

Or possibly, Picard thought, the cutting occurred immediately before her plunge and thus the blood was not dry enough when she hit the water to cling to the fabric. Here he would have help from the FBI lab.

Doc Kip reported that the complete autopsy showed no evidence of miliary tuberculosis, cancer, or any other wasting disease. Thus the riddle of her sudden loss of weight remained to plague Picard.

Vice men in the precincts were getting photographs of her made at the morgue, although her mutilated eyes would make identification difficult even if she had been a local prostitute.

Late in the day, as Picard finished his report, he raised his eyes and let them dwell on the noble elk, standing in the lake, selling life insurance from the wall calendar. He thought about his vacation for a moment. Then he forced his reverie back into the case and let his imagination play across it. But no sudden insight came. He was not the Sherlock Holmes type.

That night, in the efficiency apartment he really couldn't afford in southwest Washington, he read up on the lieutenant's examination before he went to bed. He was going to try hard this year. But it was difficult to get back to studying. He had gone to the University of Maryland for a year, then into the army. When he got out, he had not wanted to go back to college. He was sorry now. But even then studying had come hard.

He went heavily to sleep and in the night dreamed a nightmare and made a gasping attempt to cry out. If he could scream he would wake himself up and end the hideous dream, he felt. But when he did shake clear of the dream's dreadful tentacles, his scream was only a choking "ah, ah, ah."

Jesus, he said to himself, and smoked a cigarette in the middle of the night, something he seldom did. He had not had such a nightmare in years.

Morning was bright. On his desk he found a call slip from Fishbein, the Third Precinct vice officer, who said he had seen someone like the woman, yes, a bimbo, near one of the big hotels, the Santa Lucia, last summer. He'd watched her try a couple of approaches. Not enough to make a real case on her.

No, she was not just a ten-dollar streetwalker. She was dressed nice and after the two-hundred-dollar-suit trade, not a guy in a fifty-dollar ready-made. He'd seen her a couple of times on big convention nights, that was all. No, no name, but, yes, he was pretty sure it was her.

Picard walked up to the fifth floor, where the headquarters vice squad had its offices, and almost ran into Marco De Perugia, a pudgy and flamboyant detective. He would never get past detective private because he couldn't resist sampling the whores he was supposed to be prosecuting.

"I was looking for you, pickhead. I have got word for you on the doll baby which you have fished from the river."

Picard let the play on his name pass. He was used to it.

"What you got, Marco?" he said.

"No, I ain't kidding you, baby." The big vice man pulled a mug shot, a fingerprint card, and a statement of facts from his pocket and laid them in Picard's hand.

"One, two, three," said De Perugia as if showing three of a kind.

Picard looked hard at the mug shot. It was the girl.

"I could kiss you, Wop," he said tensely.

"Yeah, and get me in trouble with the pansy squad," said the morals man, smacking Picard across the shoulders, pleased with himself.

"Wilson, that's left now," De Perugia's words tumbled out, "me and Wilson busted this little lady down by the Crowley-Shelton. Wilson was bad news and no joy on this poor broad . . ."

Picard looked up from the statement of facts, quieting De Perugia for a moment with a frown. The fact sheet was couched in Wilson's policese:

"Dets. Emil P. Wilson and Marco De Perugia were approached by a female subject later identified as Sophia Adelaide Matlack W/22 of 1497 Randolph Terrace NW. at 1:30 a.m. Aug. 4, 1961, in the 1500 block of M St. NW. Subject inquired if the undersigned was lonely and on the reply of 'yes' subject suggested undersigned and Det. De Perugia visit her in the Crowley-Shelton Hotel, Room 8114. The undersigned and Det. De Perugia then placed subject under arrest. Subject was unable to give a good account of herself, had no visible means of support, and was abroad at a late and unusual hour. Undersigned charged her with soliciting for a lewd and immoral purpose."

At the top, it said "n. pped"—no papered, dropped.

"What happened? Why no papered?" asked Picard.

"I couldn't testify that that poor blonde solicited Wilson, Harry. We didn't have no case. Why, this girl made Wilson for a cop in a minute. She didn't make no suggestion to go to bed with that creep. I mean, I knew she was a bimbo, and she knew it and she knew I knew it. I mean, who don't know, Harry, that you got to have the lady lying on the bed with the money in her hand and you be standing there in your drawers to make a case, and the money marked and dunked in that purple thief powder? C'mon, Harry. The D.A. gives Wilson hell in the morning and cuts her loose and all it costs her is what the bondsman soaks her the night before."

But it had been enough to get her prints and the staring, noncommittal picture and even the hotel she frequented, and, maybe best of all, her address. It had also given her a grave with a name on it, Picard thought grimly.

"Marco, can you line me up with somebody that knew this gal? I want to talk to her." Picard paused. "I'd be taking Susy Finnerton with me."

"With Susy, Harry, how come you are interested in any of my little friends?" De Perugia asked with soft sarcasm. The remark forced a wry smile out of Picard. De Perugia continued, "Sure, Harry, sure. I'll find you a lady that knows this little dead bimbo. But you don't tell nobody here on the force how you got to her, huh?"

Picard made some routine hospital inquiries on other cases that morning, checked the D.A.'s office on a pending murder trial, and made a brief civil affidavit in a wrongful-death suit. He wanted everything out of the way.

Captain Pulanske, dripping unction, told him, "I've

cleared the decks for you, Harry. Concentrate on these two babies." Picard was glad to work exclusively on the two cases, but he was aware that Pulanske's big favor meant that he was to put in perhaps sixty hours a week.

De Perugia's word was good. He came up with the name of "Judy," a retired whore who ran a night club and who knew Sophia Matlack.

In turn, Picard called Susy Finnerton. She had been helpful on the clothing. And once she had met the whores with whom Sophia ran, once they recognized that she was not out to arrest or hamper them, she would be a valuable investigator on this case, more valuable for interviewing than a heavy-handed male detective.

That was how he justified it in his mind.

But he wondered whether this was not partially a ruse to be with her. He had known her for two years, flirting as all the detectives did with the pretty policewoman. But their frequent encounters in the last three days had stirred him and he knew it.

"Are you sure it's worth everyone's while for me to work on this thing, Harry?" she said doubtfully when he explained over the telephone how she could help.

"No," he answered her, laughing. "But it'll be more fun for you than checking out laundry markings."

"That's true enough," she acknowledged. He felt her hesitating, but sensed that she wanted to find a reason to go with him. Perhaps even in these few days he had stirred something in her, too.

"Besides, Susy, it's the only way I can get you to go out with me," he said, pressing her.

"Detective Picard," she said, agreeing to go, "I suspect your motives."

That afternoon Picard drove to the Randolph Terrace address listed on the dead whore's police record. It was a single-family dwelling now split into four apartments.

The residents were all new. The custodian-manager was uncooperative until Picard reminded him that the apartment house needed a certificate of occupancy and that this meant a fire-department inspection and that since the house was without an enclosed staircase . . .

The detective had to get only this far. The custodian, a bulky, stooped man with a bad eye, grumbled, "All right, all right, the girl was here for about six months. That was about two months ago. . . .

"Yes, well, maybe she was hustling. I guess she was, anyway, but she was quiet. The few times I saw her bring anybody in they were well dressed, middle-aged, like guys here for a convention, liquored up and playing the big shot, you know, Sergeant. . . .

"She never had no trouble with the rent, so she never had no trouble with me. Hell no, I don't run no whore-house, and if you want some evidence on that, mister, I'll take you up and show you the two bitchy old goats beginning to grow whiskers who are here now. . . .

"No, I don't know where she went to. She gave me two weeks' notice and that was that. Maybe she went to a better place."

The man asked Picard why he wanted to know all this and added, "Why, for Christ sake, don't you cops ever leave poor little hustlers alone?"

When Picard answered him, he burst out, "No! Jesus. I'm sorry. I didn't know she had been killed. She was the one they pulled out of the river? Jesus."

It was a funny sort of date he had with Susy Finnerton, he thought as he drove home to wash his Pontiac compact. But to take her to seek information from whores on one of their dead colleagues would be a welcome break for him from the lurid shootings and stabbings, sudden, meaningless suicides, and the frustrating industrial accidents that made his average day.

He picked her up at her apartment in Silver Spring, just outside of the city, at 10:00 p.m. The door was opened by a dumpy baby-sitter, introduced by Susy simply as Mrs. Kearns. He had forgotten that the pretty policewoman had a six-year-old son.

Picard and Susy drove the long way in to downtown. It was Friday night, the night Washington plays at being a big city.

Down Fourteenth Street the strip joints had crowds of sailors and flashily dressed men, pimpled and long-haired and in their early twenties, clustered around gaudy front entrances.

They bargained with the hostesses, seeking the rawest show and the lowest minimum and cover.

They passed the bright lines of globes that floodlighted the billboard of the Casino Royal. There, in huge black Gothic letters and man-high photographs a still-famous tenor shared billing with the immense breasts of an "exotic" named Telly Stahr. Down the street a block, the Aden Inn and its seraglio of belly dancers (Sandy Times, Metaxianne) lured the omphalophilic.

Inside the bars a mixed lot of no-goods, college kids, shady business punks, marginal public relations types, GIs, furtive congressmen, and expense-account bums would sit in the dark and heat up as the dollies did their work.

"I once had a broad in one of these joints advertised as Miss Billion Dollar Bust offer me another part of her anatomy for fifty dollars," he said matter-of-factly as they crossed out of the section. "It was ironic."

She half laughed, a "Hunh."

Thank God, Harry thought to himself, she isn't a complete prude.

At the Tornado Room a rock-and-roll quintet was

playing haphazardly. There was a fair crowd. It would be packed by midnight, and the quintet, souped up on sets—tranquilizers and pep pills taken together—would be swinging. Picard paid the two-dollar "door cover" and helped Susy out of her coat. She wore a conservative black dress, a jersey with a gathered skirt, that set off her figure discreetly, too discreetly for the bars they planned to visit.

Picard asked the bartender for "Judy" and the woman came from an office behind the bar wall. She was a dark woman, bulgy and forty, dressed in a good two-piece maroon suit, embellished with a little too much gold buttonry. She looked like what she was: a smart former whore who saved her money in the good days and retired to the honky-tonk business.

"Thanks for being here," he said to her as they walked to the table where Susy sat.

Judy said she had been assured by "a friend" that he was not interested in hurting her business.

"That right?" she asked cautiously.

"That's right," Picard replied as they sat down. Judy asked, and Picard told her without hesitation, why they wanted to know about Sophia Matlack—that Sophia was the woman pulled from the Potomac.

The woman cooed with surprise, then, satisfied by a whore's sixth sense that they could be trusted, she began to talk.

"Oh, I knew Sophie well, De Perugia's right about that. Nicely built girl from Kansas City or someplace. Hustling here about three years. She was dumb, but good-looking enough if you like blondes.

"Sophie, she was building up a good following as a call girl, careful and instinctive-like, you know. But she didn't have enough going for her yet to give up all the street trade. Like she'd work a convention at the Crowley-Shelton or the Santa Lucia. She'd work 'em inside or outside on the street. And don't let 'em kid you, Sergeant, a good-looking girl like that can always get herself a room inside even if she has to call first and check in later. Them big hotels like to have a pretty slut around if she don't make any trouble."

Judy said she let Sophie come to the Tornado Room anytime—even if it did mean complaints from the "regulars."

"They'd bitch about her taking their Johns away. But Sophie had some style, always wearing a pretty yellow rose on her dress. Right here on her bosom or her lapel, and always a fresh one. It was her 'sign,' you know, the fellows were crazy about it. She only fooled with the winners in here—a guy who'd buy a bottle of champagne in this place don't happen every two minutes."

When had she last seen Sophie?

"Oh, maybe four weeks ago. Sure, she looked fine, great."

Losing weight?

"Not a bit of it. She was a very healthy rosy girl."

Picard showed her the police photographs of the dead whore and Judy grunted at the stark pictures. No, she said, she did not really know if Sophie looked thinner in them. Well, maybe she was, but how could you tell with her lying half naked on a slab that way.

Enemies?

"No, not one in the world. And no boy friends. You see, she wasn't really crazy about men." Judy shrugged, puckering her lips, reluctant to talk about perversion. "And anyway, she wasn't the kind to bug a man or cheat on him in that mean way that'd make one of 'em mad enough to kill her. . . . Some nut did it. You can quote me on that," she said firmly.

Judy thought she lived someplace in old Foggy Bottom. She called over a girl who was "twisting" fluidly on the

36

small dance floor nearby with two men at the same time. The girl smiled widely at the men as she excused herself. She came to Judy looking half frightened and half belligerent.

"Honey," said Judy with a purr in her voice. "Tell the nice man where Betsy, you know, Sophie's friend, can be found right about now."

The girl, leaning over to hear Judy's soft question, exposed several superb pounds of hanging breast, but looked at Picard and hissed that he looked like a cop and she'd be goddamned if—

Judy cut her off, still quiet but no longer purring.

"Honey," she repeated coldly, "tell the nice man."

The whore flushed with anger. "Call her at LA 6-9920; she's there right now." Picard looked at Judy.

"Honey," she said calmly now. "Give her a call and tell her to be ready to see Sergeant Picard in about twenty minutes. Tell her he's from Homicide and wants to talk to her about Sophie—she got pulled dead from the river yesterday. Tell her Judy says she can talk free."

The prostitute named Betsy greeted them fearfully. She wore a wrinkled tweed skirt and looked suspicious behind her horn-rimmed glasses. She resembled a shopworn coed studying for an examination she knew she was going to fail. Her voice had the unpleasant nasal of lower-class suburban Maryland.

She had seen Sophie two or three weeks ago and frankly she had been worried about her. She had checked with a friend at headquarters (De Perugia again, Picard speculated) and he had assured her that Sophie had not been busted, that is, arrested.

The last time she saw Sophie? Well, it was a big wine and beer convention at the Crowley. They had gone up together about ten o'clock, after dinner, and Sophie got a John—a client—almost right away. Well, she had thought she would hear from Sophie the next day; they called each other most every day.

"I tried a couple of times to call her and even went by," Betsy said. "But you can't kill yourself worrying, specially when you can't do anything about it.

"The guy? Well, he talked to Sophie for a minute at that place by the new entrance where there isn't much light. You won't believe it, but I thought then that I'd of passed him. He had this stiff, funny way of walking, it just scared you. And he was a big, tall, black-dressed guy, and hunchy when he was talking to her. Forty-five, near as I could say without seeing his face, and one of those snap-brimmed hats, black, too, like George Raft in the old movies. . . . Oh, Sophie was careful. And it was just a feeling I had that this guy, all in black like he was, might be one of those whippers or wanted to get whipped and brother I just got no time at all for that kind of guy."

Betsy saw the man and Sophie get into a taxi. She guessed that Sophie took him to her place since she had no hotel room that night.

Picard, at last on the brink of a suspect's description, plucked tensely at her memory, but, however definite her feelings of distaste were about the man, the vital description remained vague.

Picard showed her the pictures of Sophie taken at the morgue, and Betsy winced. Yes, it was her, Betsy said, her coat and her dress. Yes, she did look thin. No, she wasn't on a diet. With Sophie's figure why should she be?

No diet? Picard questioned her again. He was stunned for a moment. At least subconsciously he had wedded himself to this explanation of the girl's strange wasting. Now he was bewildered.

Other friends? Betsy gave him two names and the bars where they could be found. Could Betsy give them Sophie's old address? No, she said, she truthfully couldn't remember. She would take them there. Now? The whore looked at her watch.

"Look, could we make it tomorrow?" she asked politely. "I got a big friend, a real good friend coming in about fifteen minutes and I got to get out of these tweeds. I already had to cancel one date."

She got up, indicating they should go, and answered his last question as she did: "Enemies, mister? She didn't have anything but friends."

The two bars blossomed with prostitutes, but not the right ones. Their owners, after assurances from Picard and Susy, made several telephone calls and then grudgingly gave them the girls' home addresses. But there, too, they were out.

Wearily, the two detectives got into Picard's car.

Again, as he drove Susy home, the talk turned from the case to a relaxed conversation about the force. At worst, he had found a confidant in the complex world of police politics.

"You're easy to talk to, Susy," he said frankly. "Why don't you let me take you out on a real date now that you know I don't bite." She hunched down in her side of the car, but moved no closer to him.

"Oh, Harry, office dating . . ." she started, but did not finish. He sensed that she was weakening, that she too felt at ease with him. And he did not rush her.

It was almost 2 a.m. as they drove past the Crowley-Shelton. In the cold stood a woman in a fur coat, talking dejectedly on the corner with a policeman. He lacked that air of authority a policeman assumes when he is making an arrest.

Picard, too, had walked a night beat.

Next day, Picard went alone to Sophie's house with Betsy while Susy sought the two whores they had missed the night before.

Sophie's house was off Seventeenth Street, one of those quiet little cross streets that soon would lose their dignity to interior decorators' offices and the lairs of lawyers, doctors, and dentists. He sent Betsy home in a taxi and entered the three-story Georgian building. The tenants were decidedly chilly on the subject of the dead woman.

Downstairs, a slender middle-aged man in a chamois coat greeted him suspiciously when he told him of his mission, then reluctantly invited him in. Picard sat uncomfortably on a fashionable low sofa in front of a long tile-topped coffee table that seemed too low. The man went for coffee. On the table there was a fat black book called *The Recognitions* and a sheaf of students' papers. Some kind of professor, thought Picard.

When he came back, Picard suspected that a professor was not all he was. He had the cultured low voice and the solid walk that a furtive homosexual often cultivates, and when he swayed down from the hips to put the coffee on the table, it was a giveaway.

"I gather you didn't like Miss Matlack," Picard said with just enough of the ominous to frighten the man.

Oh no, not the case at all, the professor protested. It did sort of ruin the tone of a residential street to have a tart bringing in her men at all hours of the night, he continued. But he certainly bore her no malice, no, Sergeant, far from it.

"What do you mean 'far from it'?" Picard probed.

"Well, the night she left," was the guarded reply.

"You mean you got a little?" Picard asked with dry humor.

"No, I didn't mean that," said the professor. "I mean I tried to give her a helping hand that night."

Picard's pulse quickened; when was it, two weeks ago? Three weeks ago? He pressed the man and found it was a Friday night, the same night, fifteen days ago, when the beer and wine convention was at the Crowley: the same night Betsy saw Sophie for the last time.

"Look," said Picard. "Let's just start with everything you know about that night that relates to that girl." His voice brooked no protest.

The man in the chamois jacket looked even more uncomfortable.

"I think some things are nobody's business, Sergeant. I want to be helpful, but I don't think you can order me to do what I don't care to. I don't feel you're in any position to ask me for exculpatory statements."

"Mister, you're wasting my time," Picard said sharply. "I'm not here to quibble with you. Now give. I'm not trying to make a morals case on you."

Picard stared into the man's suddenly sullen face until the professor's gaze broke. The man lifted his coffee cup, then put it down and began to talk softly.

"I have a feeling I was the last one but one to see that woman alive. I was up, never mind why—"

But Picard interrupted him with a look.

"I was up with one of my students. I heard the woman going up the stairs. I admit it, it makes me nervous every time she comes in. I keep thinking there'll be a police raid or something on her, the way she behaved." His hands fluttered in his lap.

"Well, a few moments, minutes later, I heard her come down the stairs. She walked slowly, heavily, as if she were carrying something, you know, carefully.

"I heard her drop something as she came past my door. Well, that was too much. I mean, this seemed like the last straw to me, hauling things up and down the stairs in the middle of the night.

"I opened my door, to the hallway, and her back was to me. I could see she had a suitcase in one hand, and she had just picked up a hatbox. She had a coat and some

41

dresses over her hatbox hand. It looked very awkward.

"She was all loaded up, you see, but she turned to see who had opened the door. . . . Sergeant, I do not wish to get involved in this case, in any way. I shall not get involved, and I am not involved."

He stopped, but Picard waited, tense, pitiless.

The professor started again.

"As she turned I began to formulate some rebuke for her, but it literally stuck in my throat when I saw her face. Can you imagine an expression half imploring, half mesmerized. No, that's not the way I wish to put it. She seemed to be making some mute appeal for help. I asked her, 'Are you sick?' or something silly, useless, like that. She didn't even answer. She pushed open the front door and went down the steps to a car out at the curb.

"I was shaken. I went back inside but I continued into my bedroom, where the lights were off and where I could look out without being seen. She had just thrown the clothes in the back of the car and was walking around to the other side.

"A man had stepped out and was walking around the front of the car and past the headlights. Oh, he was a gentleman, he opened the door for her as if she were some sort of queen. I saw her look back over the top of the car. It was too dark to see her expression, but I imagined it, pale, hopeless, a semi-mask as on the steps.

"Then she got into that big black car. The man walked around the rear of the automobile, got in and drove off. I told my student—yes, if you insist I shall give you his name, there is nothing wrong, nothing whatsoever—I told him that there was something evil, something terribly bad going to happen, and I was certain then, inexorably certain, that it would."

Picard waited, but that was all.

"It did happen, just as you thought," said the detective.

Bit by bit Picard had the man go back over the story. Sophie was wearing the same coat when she came down the stairs that Betsy had last seen her in. It was two hours after she had left Betsy, time enough for her boy friend and her to get in a little loving before they came back to her home, he thought.

No, the professor did not remember the license number, not all of it, but he had stared at it with that intention, to remember, and he was certain, almost certain, that the first two letters were E H and a 9 somewhere in the next three or four digits.

Well, it was just a big black car. Perhaps a Buick, or a Chrysler, or a Mercury—"all American cars these days look just the same to me," he said.

The boy friend? He had on a dark coat, yes, it could have been a chesterfield, he thought it was, and dark trousers. The hat? No, the headlights didn't light it up and there was no light by which to see the face clearly. The man had walked with great dignity, but not ponderously, not at all. Could he use the word "stalked" here. Well, he walked lightly but with dignity.

Picard got the professor's name and address and told him that he had been very helpful. He liked the professor because he had been so helpful and told him that he would try not to involve him further in the case. The man, looking at him from his pale, now weak-looking eyes, was half relieved and half dubious.

On the second floor, an alcoholic woman in her early fifties, wearing a good but dirty housecoat, answered the door. She already breathed her bane.

All that Picard got from her was that the girl had brought in too many men, that she suspected her husband of eying the woman, and, by God, if the landlord let any more prostitutes in she was going to personally call the police.

Picard left the gin smell of the apartment. He called the landlord from a pay phone in a delicatessen. There he gulped a sandwich while he waited for the man to arrive with the key to Sophie's apartment.

The landlord, dressed for Saturday in his car coat and unshaven, met him in front of the house, a little shame-faced. He had a feeling she was a bimbo when he rented to her, but she had sworn she was a secretary from St. Louis or someplace and he let her have it. She always paid on time.

The two men walked up to Sophie's third-floor efficiency apartment. It was already musty inside. The bed, which was in an alcove, was made with sharp, neat corners, although the counterpane was of sleazy rayon. The drawers were open and it was evident that Sophie had quickly selected this and discarded that in her hurry. Aside from this disorder, it was a clean, touchingly prim room.

Outside, the sun passed behind heavy clouds. The room took on a gloomy, indistinct character. Here, after all, a young woman had come, stayed briefly, and left finally for death. Was it this aspect of the room that accounted for its gloom? Picard was stirred by a strange feeling of uneasiness and looked up unconsciously for the assurance the landlord in the doorway gave him. But he too bore a look of concern.

The detective spent an hour going over the clothes, the souvenir store bric-a-brac, the tiny collection of books—cheap paperbacks about love, a paperback volume of Millay, perhaps the gift of a would-be Pygmalion—a few movie magazines, some sub-*Vogue* slicks. There were no letters, but a few cash receipts from downtown stores in the drawers, a postcard from Myrtle Beach in a woman's hand (which he pocketed). The garbage can showed two steak bones. Apparently she had eaten well when she ate. The refrigerator was full, its contents diversified. He felt the hair stir on the back of his neck.

Here was a full refrigerator. Here a girl who obviously liked food. Here was a well-built girl, made for her trade, who in little more than a week unaccountably had lost weight, lots of weight.

Picard knew instinctively that he was encountering something he had never met before, something outside all the hundreds of deaths he had investigated in the last eleven years. A great big piece of the jigsaw puzzle was missing and what he had so far was only the borders of sky at the top of the puzzle and earth at the bottom.

At the center, the puzzle was empty. What it would depict when it was filled Picard could now not even imagine.

In the bathroom wastebasket he was grateful to see only a dozen or so Kleenexes, no sanitary pads. So long a bachelor, he was delicate about such things, however incongruous it might seem in a man who daily saw death. He carefully lined up the Kleenexes in the order he took them from the basket. At the bottom of the basket was an exhausted yellow rose, and even older petals of other roses.

He carefully put the rose and petals atop a magazine and then fastidiously began to open the Kleenexes.

Most of them were balled loosely. They contained blotches of lipstick, cold-cream smears, the ordinary sort of thing that after long practice he recognized without mistake. The two most recently used pieces were dissimilar. A loosely crumpled one had a lipstick blot. The other, rolled hard as if to seal it past remembering, was difficult to open without tearing.

Picard meticulously smoothed it flat; on it were two small thin red smears about two inches apart. The smears appeared to be blood, too wide apart and too scant to have come from nostrils, too parallel to have been the tracks of a single small wound wiped twice.

The discovery was like a deep and sudden chord on a cello, important and frightening. He slipped the Kleenex between the pages of a fashion magazine. Then after a last survey of the small apartment, he told the landlord to keep the place free of tenants until the Identification Bureau could run a detailed fingerprint check on it that afternoon.

The detective drove to the FBI and arranged to have the Kleenex smears analyzed. Then he returned to headquarters, typed up his report, and went home, pondering his strange findings.

On Sunday, a team of police and Motor Vehicle Department clerks worked on the license-tag roster books of Washington, noting down black cars built since 1956 with plates carrying the letters E H, or F, which experience showed often was mistaken for E.

The motor vehicle offices in Baltimore and Richmond agreed to run their rosters too. The work was tiresome. There would be thousands of cars in the category, but it was the only substantial clue Picard had.

The dental photographs on the first dead woman had yielded nothing so far, although the dental societies of the three jurisdictions had sent out a special mailing with reproductions to members. Pulanske had won a promise from the three major national dental magazines to run the photograph.

"There may be no relation between the two broads, Harry," said Pulanske, "but we've got to assume there is. We've got to deal with it as if this bird will strike again. That's why I'm going big with it."

Picard nodded. The nationwide alert was also dramatic and made good newspaper copy. Pulanske, he thought to himself, is a political man. Then he grinned. If Pulanske made inspector, the squad would need a new lieutenant as a result of move-ups.

On the second woman, the FBI had found no blood-stains on the clothing, nor any other pertinent clue. The hack bureau had plenty of pickups at the Crowley-Shelton the night Sophie disappeared, but the drivers whose manifests showed the pickups could remember none who fitted Sophie or her male companion's description.

A small independent taxi or a driver on a commission basis pocketing the fare and keeping no record of the run—these were holes that the bureau could not fill.

In sum, the case was wide open. The only major item still out was the FBI check on the peculiarly streaked Kleenex.

It came in late on Tuesday from the Washington field office's number-two agent, not an underling, as was usual in a routine case.

"Can you come over right away, Harry?" There was none of the patronizing that sometimes tinged the tone of FBI men talking to local police. "We've got a setup in the big lab. I want you to see it. Tommy Hyde has worked it up and there's something damned funny about that sample you gave us."

Picard quickly asked, "It was blood, wasn't it?" and the agent replied cryptically, "Yes, blood, but blood plus."

Picard skipped the slow elevator in headquarters and ran down the stairs. When the FBI was excited, he knew it was worth getting excited about.

At the monumental Department of Justice he went straight to the lab and was checked through by the security man. Young Hyde, dressed in the business suit and conservative tie that are the uniform of the up-and-coming FBI agent, greeted him warmly as he entered.

In the big laboratory, a technician fiddled with an elaborate microscope-projector. For all his excitement, Picard felt embarrassed in the modern lab, the center of the elite federal police force. He thought for a moment of the old microscope in his own identification lab and sighed gently.

The white-smocked technician flicked on the projector light. It threw a fuzzy pattern of stringy lines and open spaces on the screen—a blood sample. The technician worked for a moment over his microscope and the sample came into brilliant focus.

"That's the blood," said Hyde needlessly. "Fred here says there's not a thing interesting about it. Just plain old Grade A."

The agent asked his technician to switch to the next slide.

A patch of light with vague lines—a little like an onion skin held in front of a light—came into focus. Picard said, "Spit?" and looked at the agent questioningly.

"Fred, you explain it," was Hyde's answer.

"Well, I don't really know quite what to tell you," said the technician, walking to the slide. "We found a little of this fluid, dried fluid, mixed and a little to the side of the top of each one of those smears. I treated it a little and got it under the scope and it's saliva, spit, all right.

"It's Type O. You know you can get the blood type from any of the body fluids almost. So it didn't belong to the person whose blood was on that Kleenex. That was A.

"Now the cell structure, the acid traces, I mean, there's no doubt it's spit. But we should be finding here some evidence of bacteria, evidence of dead bacteria like you'd find in an ordinary sample like this. And there isn't any. Not a bit."

Picard nodded his head incredulously. If the girl had snagged her arm on the two corners, say, of a door hinge, and then put a little spit on the nicks like anybody would, well, ordinarily something like that could explain everything. But the spit and blood were different types— and the lack of bacteria trace.

"Could you be wrong about that, about the blood types and the bacteria?" demanded Picard of the technician. The Kleenex was at least two weeks old. The sample must have been meager.

The technician was frank. He put out his hands palms up.

Yes, it was possible he was wrong on the bacteria. With a sample that way it was always possible. But, no, not on the two types.

Hyde walked Picard to the door. The FBI man was eager to help with anything that came up. Picard welcomed the younger man's enthusiasm. He envied the four extra years of school that had made Hyde an FBI man while he remained a municipal cop.

"Thanks, Tommy," said Picard. "I'll be back at you if I get anything." He started to say he wished it were a federal case so he could turn his uneasy and unanswered theories on it over to the FBI and forget it.

Five days later—thirteen days since the first body was found—the case had produced nothing to identify the first woman or Sophia Matlack's grim escort. Picard spent his days searching out independent taximen, running out the trickle of tags turned up for large black cars—the minutiae of every investigation. He had so bogged himself in seemingly fruitless detail that the details themselves had become the case.

The detective on that Sunday morning riffled through the missing-persons reports that had been coming to him from all over the country—Chicago, San Diego, Pascagoula, and on and on. That afternoon Picard called Susy at home and tried to get her to go out with him. No, she persisted, but he could feel her objections to dating a member of the force growing more and more *pro forma*. He chatted with her of the case, gossiped about headquarters, made a few light observations about her resistance to him, and finally, with what he felt was considerable grace, won a tentative date for the coming week.

Then, a skirmish lost, a battle won, he called the plump, black-haired widow of one of his old precinct friends and asked her to supper at an Italian restaurant—about three times cheaper than the one to which he had planned to take Susy.

The basket-bottomed bottle of Chianti warmed them both, draining from him the frustrations of the week. Harry liked his date, a warmhearted woman who clannishly continued to run with, and occasionally to sleep with, her husband's old comrades. It was almost 2 a.m. About time to go, the detective thought. Off in the back, he heard the telephone ring. When Mario, the owner, came to him moments later, he knew it was all up with him for the night.

"Pulanske?" he asked.

"Yep."

"Oh hell, Harry," said the woman with sympathy and annoyance.

Pulanske was politely apologetic but firm.

A woman had been pulled out of the river at Woodrow Wilson Bridge. She was dead. Her throat was cut. One big surprise: two men in a boat had seen her fall and had got her body out. When? About an hour ago. They were holding the body right there. It was either Washington's case or Prince Georges County, right on the line. Well, yes, let it go to their morgue, no problem. No identification on her, they'd have to work from the laundry markings and the clothes labels—if any—until they could get some prints. Yes, he'd better get Susy Finnerton—"You're quick enough to think of that, Harry"—to try to make a fast check on the clothing and laundry markings. And a photographer from Identification.

"By the way," said Pulanske dryly before he hung up. "You shouldn't eat at Mario's. It was the first place I called."

"Nobody else will give me credit with the lousy goddam wages, Chief," Picard said. Pulanske must be about ready for me to produce something, Picard mused as he checked his address book for Susy's number.

She was drowsy but friendly. Yes, she would get a taxi to the city line; her car was in the shop. Did he think he could have a scout car meet her at the city line? Oh, fine.

He thought of her on the other end of the line and wondered what she slept in. One of these days I'll find out, he thought with a small mixture of excitement and humor.

Picard sent his date home in a cab—to the sorrow of them both. Then he drove through the empty streets of the city and onto the expressway that took him to the new bridge.

Nine cars were parked along the Maryland side of the highway ramp. They came from Washington, the county, and Virginia and Maryland state police forces. He pulled in behind a car with North Carolina plates, a sedate Chevrolet with two-way radios that he knew came from FBI headquarters. As he strode past it he verified his guess by looking in at the flashlight in a sturdy holder, the clean interior, and the floor transmitter-receiver. The FBI turned up every time there was an interstate angle.

He looked over the parapet at the eerie scene below. It leaped out of the darkness with the clarity of a suddenly illuminated stage set. Its backdrop was the dark and rolling Potomac.

Two portable floodlights harshly lighted a roped-off area by the river. At the center of the seventy-foot semicircle of light, a beached boat, its oars haphazardly shipped, provided a makeshift catafalque for the body, bulging slightly beneath a blanket. The restraining ropes at the circle's edge were rimmed by onlookers whose white faces stood out in the glare above topcoats and housecoats, some hastily thrown over night clothes.

Near the boat Picard could see two men, Negroes, squatting patiently. Within the circle a group of six men, one in uniform, swayed in conversation while others in twos and threes spoke apart in other quadrants of the illuminated pocket.

Picard looked back from the pantomime to the road. A half-dozen cars, urged into motion by a patrolman with a red-hooded flashlight, slowly moved past the police cars. He could see other cars creeping toward the scene. Even at two in the morning, he thought, they find their way. The swarm of the curious would circle past the site like vultures kept from their prey by the patrolman until the red flashlight and the slowly rotating "cherry tops" of the police cars departed. Then the more intrepid would go down to the deserted death scene. It was the same at a fire, at a suicide, at a violent robbery.

The homicide sergeant quickly walked down the ramp to the base of the bridge and went first out of courtesy to the Prince Georges County captain in uniform. Then he walked to the boat and winced as he lifted the blanket and stared at the mercilessly floodlighted body.

The woman's blond hair was partially pushed back out of her face, narrowly framing her staring light blue eyes. Her lips were pale and the great bloodless gash that he knew had killed her stood out on her throat like a colored drawing in a medical book. This is death, the thought struck him, color me red.

There was no doubt that it was a quality death. Her coat, pulled discreetly about her body, was of Persian lamb. The water glistened on the black whorls of the full simple garment.

Through the wet hair, one silver and ceramic earring

glittered. The face was thin—Picard shuddered—too thin. What was this horror that stole the women's substance? he thought, the exhausted cadaver of Sophie replacing in his mind's eye the dead woman before him. He dug in his breast pocket for a cigarette. What had happened to them?

The facial bones were good, high cheekbones pressing out the pallid skin, which was clear, unblemished beneath the smudges of river effluvia that clung to it. He quickly noted the routine things, no rings, no calluses on her hands, no shoes, but stockings still on.

"Does she have on underpants?" he said bluntly to the county captain. "Yes," was the reply.

No rape, thought Picard. This guy gets his kicks some other way, some way tied to blood, to starvation, perhaps while he keeps them prisoner somewhere. He shook another shudder from his shoulders and walked toward the two Negroes, waiting impassive and alone.

One of them, a young man, perhaps twenty-five, was wearing a Prince Georges County police work uniform. He had three Police Department blankets around his shoulders and he calmly smoked a cigarette.

"This is the boy that got her out," said the county captain. "We didn't want you to freeze before we got you in there testifying, did we, boy?"

"No, suh," said the young man obediently.

From the two men Picard got the simple story of the recovery. They had been fishing for catfish from the boat. While they were fishing, they kept an eye on the bridge up above them. Why? Well, in case the "man" came—the police. No, they didn't think they were doing anything wrong. They just didn't want to get in any trouble.

They heard a car slow down and park up there. The lights went out and they thought it might be the "man." The older one started wrapping the rope around the starter wheel of the five-horsepower kicker just in case.

And right about then they saw something jumping off the bridge, and although it was dark there was enough moon to see it was about the size of a person, and besides what else would be coming off the bridge between midnight and one in the morning?

The man at the motor started it up, and with the river moving the person downstream they got close enough to it before its clothes began to waterlog for the young fellow to get a grip on its arm. No, suh, they didn't know when the car left, being so busy . . .

They managed to tow it out of the channel—it was just barely in the channel anyway—and got it over toward the island and still water.

But then the clothing, that's what must have made it pop up in the first place, got soaked all the way through, and down she goes right out of the young fellow's hand. But he jumped right in after it with the big catfish hook in his hand and the line unreeling from the rod in the boat and he hooked it in her coat so he could find her.

Well, he never knew that water was so salty and he hates salt water, but he gets her up off from near the bottom where she's edging along. And they loop the anchor rope around her, and using the motor and him holding her with one hand and the boat with the other, they get her around the island and into shore.

And the older man cuts over to Panorama Drive to find a telephone, while the younger man waits by the boat in the older man's coat.

Dead? Well, they reckoned she was dead when they first got to her, she being so limp. And that big cut in the neck, it had already done bleeding when they got her to shore where they could see it.

The county captain, a crude, tough man in his forties, picked up the story. The reason they came here, he said, is because this one was knocking on doors over toward

Panorama Drive and River Hill and residents that went down to answer saw him and got scared and called the police. Picard felt embarrassed for the two Negroes, who had done so well, been so resourceful. Then when they sought help from the whites, the whites had called the police on them.

"Any chance that...?" Picard nonetheless asked the captain, meaning was it possible the two fishers had killed the woman?

The man in uniform shook his head.

Picard saw Susy moving toward them from out of the circle of onlookers. He smiled and nodded. The county captain grinned a welcome and continued:

"Don't think so. They tell the same story every time. They tell it too good. We got no record whatsoever on either of these two boys. No, I don't think so at all."

Susy went to the body and deftly began to check her clothes labels. When she began unzipping the dress at the side to look for laundry marks, Picard turned his eyes back to the captain.

"You boys wouldn't kill a lady like that, would you?" the county captain asked the two men joshingly.

"No, suh," they replied seriously.

No identification, Susy said as she returned to them. Picard had expected as much, but it irritated him all the same.

Lord, Lord, he thought.

He had the Metropolitan Police photographer take pictures of her. The flashes dashed sheets of light into the faces of the growing crowds outside the ropes. Two Washington reporters and three photographers were shouting at Picard from outside the ropes.

No, he shook his head, they couldn't come into the area. The uniformed men hustled them back when, despite his nod, they tried to enter.

The county captain shouted his approval at his officers. The newspaper photographer and the two television cameramen shot despondently from behind the ropes.

"We keep 'em in their place out here," said the captain. Picard smiled wearily. In political Washington it was different. The press could not be offended.

The police photographer had finished his first series. Then Picard asked Susy to comb the woman's hair out of her face so the policeman could take more pictures. These would go to the newspapers to pacify them, and perhaps to aid in identifying the woman.

He walked beside Susy to the body, and as she hesitated a moment, he deftly closed the corpse's eyes with his fingers. Susy used her own comb on the woman's hair, then discarded it on the ground. Reconsidering, she stooped and picked it up and carried it to the river, where she threw it in with an underhand toss.

The photographer finished his "beauty" shots and joined Picard and Susy, his old Speed Graphic in his hand, as natural there as if it were an appendage. Picard would have liked to keep going on the case. But he was growing terribly tired. He knew he should get the question of whose case it was out of the way, but he thought, I'm too tired. It's not my problem. Let the officials iron it out tomorrow. As long as nobody fools with that body, let it go to their morgue.

"Let's go, Susy," he said. "Ready, Mike?" he asked the photographer. They walked to the top of the ramp, and the photographer loaded his equipment into his cruiser and waved at them as he pulled into the line of cars still circling past the scene.

A county cruiser's light rotated as they walked toward Picard's car. The red light showed on Susy's features, red, then darkened, red, then darkened, red . . .

The face, Picard noted, was not as young-looking as

when it was made up during the day. But it was a good, regular face with the wrinkles beginning in the right places.

She stopped at the bridge railing and looked down. Off to the southeast the river was dark and a cool breeze came upstream from the sea and touched them. Almost directly below, the floodlights still made a raw and startling island in the dark.

Picard gently took her arm as they turned away, knowing that she knew he was aware she needed no such guidance. But for this very reason she did not stop him. It flicked across his weary mind that this was her surrender to him, or agreement or acceptance or whatever the act of submission is to be called in women. His pleasure was deep, momentary, and anticipatory. Something, quite silently, had been decided between them.

They drove briefly along the river, then cut east rapidly past the flashing caution lights and on down the gray canyon of Sixteenth Street. The coming dawn had lightened the sky to eastward. They could see it, gray, clouded, as they passed the cross streets of the big avenue.

"She'll have clothes too big for her, and no marks and be just like the other one, Susy," said Picard. "And Christ knows who she'll turn out to be and we're no better off than we were." He stopped his complaint. "Can you give us a hand on the clothes again?" he asked.

Susy leaned back against the seat. She made no answer. He thought she might be asleep and looked over at her quickly. She was pensive, but her eyes were open. She's got a good profile, he thought, looking at her face, in which there was little softness.

Without turning toward him, she said quietly but matter-of-factly, "You're tired, aren't you?" Then before he could answer she added, "Harry, you're a good man, and you give them their money's worth."

Picard pulled the car to the side of Sixteenth Street and

cut the lights, no longer needed anyway in the dim dawn. He turned and kissed her with no hurry and not much passion, but with warmth—and respect. She let herself be kissed, then returned his kiss. She broke away mildly.

"I've got to get back to the boy and relieve Mrs. Kearns," she said. Picard continued looking at her. She smiled at him and touched his hand as he turned on the ignition and started the car.

"I should get out of this business," he said with a little bitterness as the car accelerated. "This is no way for anything like this to begin."

In the morning, at the funeral home in Riverdale which doubled as a county morgue, Picard and Susy found the body as they had expected—no marks of violence except for the great jagged wound in the throat. At two points near the wound there were yellowish bruises—or what looked like bruises.

The Maryland medical examiner suggested that the bruises predated the cut, but had no explanation for them. They were slight in any case. The doctor told them the woman appeared "markedly cachectic, but the cancer, acute leukemia or miliary tuberculosis that this brings to mind simply is not present."

Picard stared at the man, who smiled back nervously.

"Cachexia: she's wasted away," he explained.

"Yeah, I just hadn't heard it put that way," said Picard.

Picard asked if he would call Doc Kip in to compare notes, and the medical examiner willingly agreed. He seemed out of his depth.

The old coroner arrived and made his examination. He thought for a minute or two before he spoke.

"Harry," he said. "This woman didn't lose all that blood naturally. She was drained almost as thoroughly as if a good embalming job were done on her.

"This little lady very likely would have died of starvation if the bleeding hadn't killed her. There was that radical a weight loss," the coroner added.

The detective waited for him to speculate, and when he did not, Picard pressed him. But the coroner shook his head. "I just don't know," he said.

Doc Kip asked Susy about the clothes. The dress was a Chanel and the bra a Marja, and yes, they were too big.

"Do the papers know about the clothes in these cases being too large, Harry?" questioned Doc Kip, and Picard nodded "No."

"Then," said the coroner, "don't tell them."

Picard looked at him curiously, but he shook his head again and Picard sat back in a chair with his own grim thoughts.

The coroner and medical examiner agreed that she had been killed—or died—four to eight hours before she was flung into the river. There was no evidence of rape, or indeed of recent intercourse.

There was no doubt in the detective sergeant's mind that the new case was murder, and that the killer also had murdered Sophie and probably the first woman, too. And perhaps others not yet discovered. But what sort of murderer was it?

Deranged, of course, one who got no thrill from rape or the ordinary perversions. The Christie murder case in England crossed his mind: sex and death. But here it was starvation. Why?

While he sat waiting for the coroner and the medical examiner to sign their preliminary reports, an employee of the funeral home brought him an urgent message. He was to call a number immediately.

The phone rang once. A male voice was on the other end.

The man was a night government employee, never

mind where or what his name was, he said. As the talk developed Picard recognized him as one of the thousands of decent, humdrum middle-class citizens who continue to believe that they have a civic duty when circumstances force them to it.

The man, choosing between silence and convenience, on the one hand, and speaking out and domestic problems, on the other, first told Picard that he wanted to help if Picard would keep his name out of it. Picard agreed tentatively.

Well, said the man, who explained he was at a pay station, he had told his wife he was on overtime this morning—you see, he worked the 2-10 p.m. trick. But in fact he had cut down to a craps and blackjack joint near Hunt's Corner, something he did maybe once a week.

Anyway, he continued, he was crossing the bridge toward Virginia at about twelve-thirty this morning and he saw a big black car, a Chrysler, fairly late model, maybe a big Dodge, with its lights out, pulled up to the side of the bridge headed toward Washington. That is downstream, yes.

Well, he slowed down at first to see what was the matter with the car, but it was late, so he sped up and kept going. As he pulled across the bridge he could still see the car in his rear-vision mirror.

At the Virginia end of the bridge, he stopped and looked back, feeling guilty for not seeing what was wrong with that car. Then the lights went on and the car headed toward D.C. So he felt all right about it, that is, until he read about the murder in the first edition of the *News* today. Well, the poor girl, he just—

License plates? No, he didn't think of that. It was a good big car, looked like a medium-sized Chrysler, nope, not an Imperial, he knew that one. Maybe a big Dodge sedan. No, hell no, he didn't want to come down and look at car models. He'd sneaked out of the house to make the call already. . . .

Well, he finally assented, if it was such a key clue. But why couldn't it wait until his lunch hour from the Government Printing Office at about 6 p.m.? Now?

Oh, what the hell, he'd tell his old lady the whole thing and be down in about a hour. Maybe telling would help him break the gambling habit—that is, if his wife left anything of him when she found out.

Picard's spirits rose. He was walking back to the room where Doc Kip and the medical examiner were giving a cautious briefing to the reporters, when one of the funeral home people caught him again.

It was headquarters this time, Pulanske. He was to come in fast. They, he and Pulanske, were to meet with the chief and some diplomat, Pulanske didn't know who, in forty-five minutes.

In the antechamber of the chief's office, both he and Pulanske felt ill at ease. Picard stared at the plaques and trophies that the old man had won years ago as an Olympic revolver shot, then the phone buzzed and the willowy desk lieutenant ushered them in.

Chief Matthews had come a long way from dodging the brickbats of the bonus army. Picard noted the snifters in the chief's and his guest's hands, and the squat cognac bottle on the table. Behind the immense desk, a photograph of the new President was flanked by pictures of the two District-affairs Congressional chairmen—all graciously endorsed and signed.

The chief and his obviously nervous guest rose from the cluster of leather easy chairs in the center of the room, and the chief put his arm around Pulanske.

"Your Excellency, Captain Pulanske and Sergeant Picard. They are handling this case for me." The men shook hands as the chief explained that "Ambassador Heldwig is head of the Scandian economic and military mission attached to the embassy."

The chief poured the two detectives drinks from the Remy Martin bottle without asking them what they wanted. Picard could feel the diplomat studying them.

The chief gently advised the detectives that His Excellency had seen the girl's picture in the newspaper and then more pictures at headquarters. The girl, he said even more softly, was his daughter.

Picard risked a glance at the diplomat. His youngish face was pale beneath a shock of gray-blond hair. He must have got a jolt from those pictures, Picard thought grimly.

"Harry," the chief said in the warm, brisk voice that had helped carry him so far, "I want you to make sure that there are no reporters around when the ambassador goes to Prince Georges County—to the funeral home for final identification."

"Captain," he said, investing Pulanske's title with great dignity, "I want you to afford the ambassador any of our investigative facilities. I am also making arrangements for the FBI to help out wherever possible within their statutory grant of authority.

"I have explained that until an interstate angle has developed, the FBI cannot step in, however much both the ambassador and myself would like it. Prince Georges and I decided this morning that it was a Washington case."

Picard could hear the hint of a leer in the chief's well-modulated voice. It was clear that the chief, smelling an early solution and consequent fame, had thwarted the ambassador's wish that the case be discreetly handled by the FBI. The police politicking was a mirror of the greater and subtler wheeling and dealing on Capitol Hill and in the huge executive departments.

Picard would pick up the ambassador that evening in

a plain headquarters cruiser and take him to the funeral home after ascertaining that the press was gone. This simple arrangement—without captains, kings, and State Department protocolists—would ensure the maximum in discretion.

The four men walked through the chief's anteroom to the elevator, and Pulanske gently asked whether His Excellency could discuss some of the details surrounding his daughter's disappearance.

Heldwig started, then smiled sallowly. He told Pulanske stiffly that he could say little, really nothing. The elevator came, the chief shook hands all around. The operator dropped the elevator to the street floor without stopping for other summonses.

Outside, the ambassador's car waited. Pulanske again asked whether anything came to His Excellency's mind that might be helpful in apprehending . . .

The envoy began to cut him short again, then spoke hurriedly.

All that he knew, he said, was that she left their home in Chevy Chase to visit friends in Philadelphia. No, he did not know their names. She was twenty-four and did what she pleased. And that was the last he had seen of her. Yes, he said, looking curiously at Pulanske, now that he had mentioned it she did appear thin in the photographs.

But when Pulanske sought to use these bare words as a wedge to details of the girl's background, the envoy said, "I don't think I can add anything to that." His chauffeur officiously handed him into the back seat and then drove the shiny Humber toward embassy row on Massachusetts Avenue.

"There's something smelly in Scandia, Harry," said Pulanske. "I don't buy that visit to Philadelphia stuff. God, that guy could be helpful if he wanted to."

Pulanske asked Picard to call him when the identification was positive. He, Pulanske, would release it from home to the press.

"Funny, he didn't want to go to Riverdale right now and make it certain," Picard observed.

"He knows once he makes it certain we got to release it to the press," said Pulanske. "And one thing these cool babies don't want is this kind of publicity. This thing has a smell to it somehow, and I'll bet it winds him up in Timbuktu or Sydney, Australia, or some other God-awful place studying culture exchanges instead of drinking no-tax hooch and chinning at the White House."

The two detectives walked back into the huge pillbox of a building. Pulanske told him the case was getting two junior men from Homicide, plus senior detectives from the sex, general assignment, and auto squads. Pulanske could ask for more men as he needed them.

"The chief wants some kind of solution fast," he said. "You got your work cut out, Harry. I'm getting everybody together upstairs now." The Scandian girl's murder had put the case in the big league.

Picard had worked these joint teams before. On this one Pulanske would be the nominal head and he, Picard, would be doing much of the work. But Pulanske's role had two edges. True, a solution would redound to Pulanske, but a failure would too.

Upstairs Pulanske called together what the newspapers called a "supersquad." They assembled, some carrying the late editions of the *News* headlined "POLICE SEEK NAME OF MURDERED BEAUTY" and overlined *"New Potomac Mystery."* The girl's face, eyes closed, took up the rest of the page, except for a cutline beginning in bold face "DO YOU KNOW HER?" It was a classic murder case as far as the papers were concerned—because it sold papers.

Pulanske briefed them, concisely and fully, a real pro, Picard thought, when he's not hamming it for inspector.

The homicide captain warned that anyone who leaked the name of the new girl before the ambassador made his identification was on the way back to the precincts.

He outlined what they had to work with:

The killer liked blondes, plump ones; yes, the Scandian girl was plump and blond. No, he didn't know whether the first girl looked like a hooker and the second was a hooker and the Scandian girl, whatever she was, wasn't a hooker.

They would want to send out all points on missing blondes—open and closed cases—during the past year. The guy was a crackpot, so open up the no-rape killer files, find out who just got out of the prison at Lorton and the criminal kook ward at St. Elizabeths.

They'd want the FBI to give them whatever help they could on the pervert files. Pulanske quickly shuffled through his papers and continued.

There were about two dozen calls that might have some bearing on the black car—calls from late night travelers, anonymous sensation seekers wanting even a furtive and destructive part in the case, overheard threats, "cases I remember."

The auto files looked better now as a source of information, Pulanske noted. This Printing Office employee's tip looked good for making the car a Chrysler or big Dodge. They'd want to step up and narrow the search and give Baltimore and Richmond a goose on the Maryland and Virginia auto checks. Yes, and the taxi manifests should be run again.

The first dead woman's deteriorated body had been cremated, but a Baltimore medical mannikin firm had processed the skull. He had detailed diagrams and photographs now of the teeth. He, Pulanske, would call the three city editors and see if this dental stuff could run and if the AP and UPI would carry it.

Would Robley from General Assignment try to get the

lads in the vice squad working hard to come up with something from their bimbos? Yes, he could hint at a transfer to the detective squads for a good solid clue. Oh, and they'd want to question the professor and the college kid that was with him, Betsy the whore, the two Negroes, the whole bunch again, just in case they forgot anything.

The whole list of that beer and wine convention the night Sophia Matlack disappeared should be run against the FBI files to see if any funny ones are on it. Fritz from the auto squad could check out the cars with their home states.

When he had finished with the briefing, Pulanske went to Picard's desk, sat on it, and talked quietly to his aide.

What did Harry think, Pulanske said, about working a decoy angle. They were getting a pattern, you know.

Picard looked up curiously. Pulanske continued:

"Look, Harry, all these gals were blond. All, like I said, plump. I'd guess the first girl for certain a whore, otherwise something surely would've turned up on her. This Sophie was a whore. That ambassador ain't kidding me either. That daughter of his was up to something.

"When we make out where the Scandian gal was last seen, I'm gonna want to think about putting some bait out. I mean some well-protected bait . . ."

"You're talking about Susy," said Picard glumly.

"Right," said Pulanske. "She doesn't look like a whore," he said, grinning a bit cruelly at Picard. "But she's blond and she isn't skinny, at least to look at her. She could get dressed up like a slut. I mean, hell, think how many cases we've made with stake-outs. I had Susy in the same kind of rig once on an abortion case, you probably remember it."

Pulanske got off the desk.

"I'll talk to her when the time comes," he said, and slapped Picard on the shoulders. "Buck up, she's not your wife, you know. Feel her out on it if you want to, you'll be seeing her at that screwball funeral today, won't you?"

"Yes," said Picard thoughtfully.

The funeral was Sophie's. Picard was heading the detail. With the publicity of the new death, Sophie could count on a good send-off from the curious.

The prostitute had barely escaped potter's field. Mike Mockley, a feature writer for the *Star*, had done a poor-unwanted-whore article on how Sophie was to be given a bleak indigent's burial after cremation by the morgue. Betsy called Picard the afternoon of the story and asked him hesitantly if he could have Sophie buried in a real graveyard.

Not him, said Picard. But you can do it if you can get together whatever it costs. Nobody had claimed the body, so any friend could assume custody.

Betsy had come to Homicide, wearing her prim tweeds and a frightened look and carrying fifty dollars and a promise to have some more from other girls by the next day.

The paper also received contributions and an offer from a Baptist minister in Fairfax to let Sophie lie in his church-yard. More important to Picard, a fifty-dollar bill clipped to Mockley's story came to the *Star* from Baltimore. The address on the five-and-dime envelope was typed on a Hermes portable. There was no other clue to the sender.

It could have been a "John" who had enjoyed the pros-titute, or a crank, or the killer perhaps, Picard thought. It was one more small mystery in a bag full of big ones.

The church was on the outskirts of Fairfax City, near Washington, its site in woods just off the highway. The new brick building was already surrounded by parked cars when Picard got there. The Fairfax police had not antici-pated the crowd and a king-sized traffic jam had set in.

Picard saw that it was going to be a carnival. The bright warm afternoon did not help. Teen-age kids were loitering around the church. They mugged in front of the police cameraman assigned by Picard to shoot the arriving cars for possible clues. The police were too busy to help.

A man in a seamless old overcoat was passing out repent-in-haste tracts. Picard took one and passed it to Susy with a lemon-peel smile. It was from a Washington evangelist group.

"Be saved, Susy," he said.

The young Baptist minister who had naively made the offer of his graveyard watched nervously as the curious who had flocked to his church trampled his newly laid lawn, his incipient flower garden. The crowd was all white, Picard noted, but did not ponder why. He was a detective, not a sociologist.

Picard stood with Susy watching the unruly throng. She seemed uneasy, withdrawn.

"What's the matter with you?" he asked her.

"We're using this case to see each other," she said. "I was a damned fool to ever let myself get interested in this," she added testily.

"You want out?" he said, irritated himself from too little sleep, too much officialdom, and too few really good leads.

"No, Harry," she replied more mildly.

Inside, the minister gave a saccharine talk on the throwing of the first stone. It had a fraudulent ring that annoyed Picard.

He stood by the wall in the front of the church on the opposite side from the minister and looked at the communicants. He tried to fix in his mind the faces of the grown men. All too many of them looked like oddballs.

Only the four prostitutes from the District looked sincere. They had paid their money, invested in the ceremony—suggested the idea of having a yellow rose laid in the coffin. They had dressed conservatively, almost dowdily.

The service was brief. Sophie was buried in a far corner of the churchyard as the police fought back the crowds who pushed in—silent, but relentless—to get the last look at the coffin.

Picard and Susy saw the reporter Mockley contribute to the poor box as they walked in the church after the ceremony to see whether the minister had gotten any kook calls. Mockley gave the three of them a weak, slightly sick smile. He had met Picard several times while working on the feature about Sophie.

"Never a sparrow falls," he said to Picard. The minister looked up, saw the slight sarcasm in Mockley's face, and reddened with anger. Mockley stared him down, then exited with a mock sign of benediction.

Outside, Susy diligently sought to draw a remembrance from the four prostitutes of anyone similar to the tall, dark man who was seen with Sophie. But although they tried to be helpful, Susy's talk brought no solid clue.

Picard went back with Susy to the grave after the last of the curiosity seekers, the press, the police photographers, the officers and detectives had gone. They were all alone in the trampled corner of the large graveyard. Dusk was coming on and the warm breeze of afternoon had turned to a chill April wind. It soughed in the pines nearby, lifting and dropping scraps of paper left by the crowd that had marched across the raw earth beside the grave.

"Where do you suppose he will hit next?" Picard said almost to himself. Susy probed a tuft of early grass with the pointed toe of her pump.

"Where did he hit last time?" she asked.

"I don't know," he replied. "That Scandian diplomat knows more than he wants to say. Funny the killer would hit somebody bound to bring on a big effort like this diplomatic girl, when the first time he hit girls that nobody cared if they were alive or dead."

"Maybe," said Susy, "he made a mistake. Maybe he didn't know what he had on his hands."

They walked back toward the parking lot in the growing gloom. The wind cut through their light topcoats. The sun, already behind dark gray clouds that had come up fast with the wind, was westering and setting without display. Picard did not try to touch her and she did not encourage him. Now there was something stilted and "on duty" between them.

"Pulanske is going to ask you to play decoy," Picard said abruptly. "You know, have you hoofing around where this guy got Sophie with a bunch of detectives on hand in case anything happens."

She looked at him, surprised, then kept walking.

"I guess he thinks I've been in training, talking to all these women," she said in a small voice.

He patted her shoulder awkwardly but did not try to take her hand.

"You might get to like the life," he said in an attempt at lightness. She said she doubted that, and left it at that.

He drove her to Silver Spring.

"Try to get some rest," she said as she left him, looking at him with warmth for the first time since they went to the funeral.

Picard drove back to headquarters, shaved there, and polished his shoes. He ate three packages of cheese crackers, drank a Coke, and then went down to get the captain's homicide cruiser. It was shined carefully for his meeting with Ambassador Heldwig.

In the military-economic annex of the embassy a minor functionary led Picard to Heldwig's office, where the diplomat sat in an easy chair, reading papers through half-moon glasses. They made him look older and even more tired than he had appeared earlier in the day.

The man left and Heldwig asked Picard to sit.

"I am not anxious to go, Sergeant," the diplomat sighed. "I have no doubt at all that it is she." Picard did not reply. Heldwig was now obviously reflective.

"You knew I was not telling you the whole truth, as you say, this afternoon," he continued. "I am prepared to do so now. I do not wish to stay here in Washington longer, and the scandals of a departed diplomat's family are of little moment."

Heldwig got up and put on his coat. Picard drove them toward Riverdale. All the way Heldwig was silent, watching the street lights go by, and Picard did not press him.

Only the Prince Georges County detective captain and the owner of the funeral home were there when they arrived. The four men walked through a side door and into the antiseptic cleanliness of a small room where three bodies lay.

The captain nodded at the body in the center, under a clean canvas sheet. The funeral official stepped forward with nervous alacrity. He pulled back the sheet from the girl's face, then quickly let it drop.

Heldwig bent slightly over the pale face and turned back to the three men. His face was pasty white. His eyes rolled up as if he were going to faint and the two detectives rushed forward and got him by the arms.

The Prince Georges captain grabbed a small brandy bottle from the hand of the funeral director, who had efficiently produced it from an inside pocket of his coat.

"Here," said the Maryland policeman. Rather roughly he shoved the half-pint bottle toward the man's chest. The diplomat freed his arm from Picard's grasp and bolted a swallow. He coughed and the two detectives sat him down in a folding chair also produced by the undertaker.

Heldwig put his head in his hands for a moment. When he looked up, his face was tired, a blank mask.

"Could we go now, Picard?" he said. The Washington detective walked with him from the little morgue room and at a desk outside the diplomat signed the papers certifying the identity of his daughter for the police.

"Captain, I want to thank you for the drink," he said to the Maryland officer. "I know, of course, you have your obligation to the press. But I would appreciate it so much if you could give them only the name, my position and the bare details of my visit. And could you tell them I will not be available for their calls?"

As he spoke he shook the big policeman's hand and looked into his eyes.

"Your Excellency, I'll do everything I can on this," said the county captain emotionally. Heldwig's control had impressed them, and both the captain and Picard were touched.

Driving back through the garish county suburbs that festered with neon light alongside the road, Heldwig began his story. Picard drove silently, letting the tale come out. He would have questions, but they could wait until the gravamen of the matter was told.

"I came here five years ago. My wife was dead," said Heldwig quietly. "I brought my daughter." He stopped suddenly and turned to the detective. "I depend on you, Picard, to use only what you need of this to catch your killer. I depend on you to keep my confidences, from even your superiors on those matters which are not germane to your case—in so far as it is permissible, of course . . ."

He shook his head as if shrugging off a bitter draught.

"*Ach,* in any case, someone would talk, someone start the ugly chain of gossip as they always do in your country.

"My daughter had two abortions, two that I know of, in my country. Yes, I know what you must be thinking of

72

what they say about the morals of my country—of what we exemplify for the world in this regard. But in fact this so-called promiscuity, if you will, can be a healthy boy-girl thing. Not so with Norma. With her it was almost a disease, that is to say, with her, men were almost a disease. But, I have the feeling she did not really enjoy sex. If I am to believe what she says she told her psychiatrist—yes, oddly we had our communications—there was a compulsion, nonetheless. I suspect in a way it was to punish back somehow. That no doubt is how the Freudians would have it.

"After we came to this country, for a while, the whirl of parties, the idea of being perhaps the loveliest girl in the foreign colony here, this seemed enough to keep her interested. It served to forestall the re-emergence of her problem."

The diplomat smiled sadly.

"Our problem," he corrected himself.

"But it did not last. First there was an affair with one of your bright young Congressional people, then a series of affairs. And in the last year, worse, horribly worse, she began to do what she did, pay me back, whatever it was . . ."

Heldwig was talking rapidly now.

"Yes, yes, you want to know what I mean by worse. . . . Nominally she lived in our house at Chevy Chase. But only nominally, Sergeant. In fact, she had an efficiency apartment at the Chapman House. Often I did not see her for a week at a time. She has—had, I'm sorry—a small income from her mother's estate. But when she did visit me, it was for still more money—money I gave her. It was thus that I bought these few visits. And I gave her pathetic little warnings.

"What was she doing? I shall tell you, Picard. She was playing the whore. I mean it literally. Through an old friend here, an old, old friend, a lawyer, I hired a private detective.

"The detective found she was making dates by telephone. You refer to them as call girls here. She entertained four, five, even six men in an evening at times.

"Mercifully, she used a false name at the Chapman House, this decency at least, she observed.

"She went out occasionally to the big hotels, with dark glasses on, but as a streetwalker. I might myself have encountered her when I left receptions at the Santa Lucia or the Crowley-Shelton."

The big downtown hotels! This is where Sophie was picked off. This, too, then could be where the killer encountered the Scandian girl, Picard thought.

"I had considered sending her home," the envoy continued in his dry, tired voice. "But she is an adult. She did not want to go, not that she liked it so here, I suppose. It was just inconvenient for her to move and she indulged her convenience.

"That concludes my story. The visit to Philadelphia was a fraud, of course. I did not know where she went. Had I not seen her picture in the paper, I should have checked the hotel for her, perhaps today, just to see that she was still alive. No doubt they are accustomed to calls for her from unknown men."

The diplomat looked bleakly out of his window, then turned to Picard.

"I hope you can be discreet. I am thinking, of course, of myself, but also I am thinking of her, her wretched, pitiable life and death."

Picard satisfied the diplomat of his own discretion, and at first gently, then, as he felt the diplomat's weakness, more firmly, he questioned him about the girl.

Her lovers? The report from the private detective had named a few, but all were unknown to Heldwig. Yes, he would provide Picard with a copy of the report.

Her eating habits? She ate well, Heldwig began, and

once more Picard felt the sensation of dread and excitement, of awe, that accompanied the paradox of women who ate well in life and appeared starved in death.

"She drank too much," Heldwig was saying. "And smoked too much, but however ill she may have been mentally, she ate well, always, nothing touched her appetite. To have been so thin, why she must have starved herself in the last two weeks or so, or been starved. . . ."

The detective, haunted by the victims' thin bodies, pulled up before the embassy, and the diplomat made his uncomfortable adieus before disappearing inside.

At the Chapman House, later that night, the weary detective got his first big break. Picard knew the house detective, both from the man's previous service on the force and from the several suicides and other deaths that had marked the hotel's short but colorful existence.

The heavy-set house detective, formerly a general-assignment sergeant, located the bellhop who had carried Norma Heldwig's bags from her room when she left the hotel for the last time, a little more than a week before.

The house detective told Picard that he had no doubt what Norma, known to him as Frances DuBoyard, was up to. But she paid her rent on time and was quiet about her men. They were always well dressed—if a little high—when they arrived. She drove a Porsche. And the house detective always figured her as sort of psycho.

"Mickey," he told the bellhop, a wiry little man of about forty who looked like a white chimpanzee, "Mickey, we ain't going to kid Sergeant Picard about nothing, understand. You ain't going to get in any trouble if you level, only if you hold back. Then you will be in big trouble, Mickey."

The bellhop nodded acquiescence, but neither fear nor real obedience showed in his small dark eyes. Yes, he said, he certainly did remember the last night Miss DuBoyard was there. You goddam right he remembered.

The desk had sent him back to her room. She rented it in the monthly apartment section, looking out on the park.

He had knocked and she said sort of weakly, "Come in." He saw right away from the mess the apartment was in that she was in a hurry about something. Miss DuBoyard was bent over, putting a dress in her suitcase.

"Oh, she had a fine full rump, she did," he exclaimed. "Lord, she never needed no kind of girdle and—good looking legs, you better believe it. Well, she closes the suitcase, which is on the bed with a matching piece, no two, there was a hatbox, too."

The bellhop stopped for breath.

"She turns around and she looked pale as hell, so I says to her, 'Anything the matter,' but she just gives me a sick-looking smile and says, 'Unh uh.' I think she must be high, not on hooch with a look like that, but on H—heroin— except I never had no reason to think she used the stuff.

"Besides I've seen her tossing down them brandies and water in the hotel bar, and you don't see a snowbird tossing down juice like that.

"So, I take the bags down the hall, thinking about her looking funny, but still a classy broad and I wouldn't mind taking a crack at it if I could."

Mickey's words tumbled out.

"When we get outside the hotel I don't see any car in the driveway, then she says quiet like, 'Right over there, the car over there.' And it isn't her Porsche, it's a big Dodge. Yeah, yeah, I'm sure it's a Dodge. I'll get to that. The Dodge is parked off the driveway in that little lot.

"So I think, what kind of scum that won't pull his car up in front of the hotel, or else he's mighty worried about the missus finding out he's with a hustler, or something. I get the bags up to the car and I see this guy in the front seat, the guy is looking straight ahead.

"Oh, but he is a weirdo, dark as it is I can see he's got one of those skinny long straight noses, and a long ugly face. He's wearing a black snap brim hat and a black coat with the collar turned up, you see.

"The back door is open, but I'm thinking only of putting the bags in the trunk, so I say, 'You got the key, sir? I'll put these in the trunk.' Miss DuBoyard is already around the car and is opening the front door herself, the jerk not even getting out to open it, when he says, 'Put the bags in the back seat.'

"Now that is all he says, but there is something in that voice that I won't forget in a million years.

"It's a deep voice, slow, coming from way back in the throat like an animal's growl. And tired, very tired.

"But I tell you, Sergeant, there was something in that voice that was like if you didn't do what he wanted you to he would kill you in some awful way—just as soon as look at you, like somebody would strike a match to light a cigarette."

So the bellhop pushes the bags into the back seat and automatically starts to the front for a tip, but the car is already in gear and he has to move back fast to keep from being brushed.

"The guy has some kind of funny accent, it ain't Jewish or Italian and it ain't Nigra or Southern and those are the only kind I can tell. Anyway, I think with the accent the guy must be some big gun from some embassy not wanting anybody to know he's picking up some bimbo, even a sharp chick like Miss DuBoyard, or whatever her real name is."

So Mickey, the bellhop, looks at the license as the Dodge drives off, and even as dark as it is and no moon to speak of, he can see by the driveway lights that the car doesn't have DPL plates, just plain D.C. plates. And that's how he knows it's a Dodge because there it is right on the trunk: D O D G E.

"Listen, Sergeant, I said Dodge, '60 or '61, and black or dark blue and I'd testify to it. When a car damn near nips you, you don't forget what it looks like, do you?"

It was midnight. The house detective and the bellhop took him to the dead girl's room. A chambermaid apparently had straightened it. There was little interesting at first glance except the leather-framed picture of her father as a younger man inside the top drawer of her dresser. And a package of contraceptives in the closet under the towels.

Picard asked the house detective to keep the room locked. He called Pulanske to tell him briefly what had happened. At the homicide captain's suggestion, he called Fritz of the auto squad, jarring him from sleep. He told the auto squadman that the car was definitely a Dodge, probably '60 or '61, and had Washington plates. Fritz said that he would call the Detective Bureau desk lieutenant and try to get one of the overnight guys off the street. He could weed the Dodges out of the Washington license lists they had drawn up.

"Jesus, Harry, we're not looking for the needle in the haystack any more. Even figuring since 1959, there can't be more than two thousand black Dodges in D.C.," said Fritz.

Picard wanted to call Susy. He wanted to talk about his case. It was on the tracks now and soon or late they were going to have the name of a good suspect. He wanted to quicken her with his excitement, share it. But he was not a precipitate man, only a dogged one. So he passed up the possibility of tying her closer to him with a confidence. And instead he began the long drive through town to his apartment in southwest Washington.

By noon the next day he knew how far among Washington's two hundred thousand cars he would have to look.

Fritz and Picard computed that there were four hundred to seven hundred 1960 and 1961 Dodges that weren't taxis, with a maximum of two hundred having one of the three possible letters based on the professor's clues. This was a manageable number. And if the professor were right about the 9 he saw in the plate, the total would be perhaps seventy.

But the owners of these two hundred could be weeded from the massive tag-listing books only by hand. When the police or motor vehicle clerks produced a possibility, the name was quickly called in to the supersquad for forwarding to the FBI and a check against the agency's millions of criminal records.

That night, Picard went to Susy's apartment for dinner. It was the first time she had asked him and he had a bottle of good red wine under his arm and his best suit and manners on.

Her boy, Bernard, was up when he came in, and was dressed in a little coat and tie. Picard knew that it would have been easier to have the child in pajamas. He was pleased at Susy's gesture and touched. She had on a dark brown shirtwaist dress, trim on her neat figure, and her hair was drawn back prettily behind her ears.

"You look like you're bucking for a promotion, Susy," he said as he walked in. She laughed and thanked him for the wine. And while he was saying hello to the little boy—before he had time to feel nervous—she had a martini in his hand and he was at ease.

"Mummy says you're a good detective," the boy said. "Do you watch Eliot Ness?"

"Yes," said Picard. "He's good, isn't he?"

"I don't know," said Bernard. "Mummy won't let me watch him." He was a nice child, more delicate than Picard would have expected from his father. When Picard had prattled with him enough to like him but to wish he would go to bed, Susy took him in.

Picard glanced around the apartment, one of thousands like it in the suburbs: two bedrooms with a small living room, a dining alcove, and a pinched kitchen on the second of four floors, an apartment costing perhaps a hundred five dollars a month. Susy had decorated it with bright modern landscapes and rich-looking curtains. The women he ordinarily went with had apartments almost indistinguishable from it in size, but they widely missed Susy's style.

"Susy, you didn't get your taste from those Seventh Street shoplifters you spend your time with," he said, wishing he could be clever, sharp. He was acutely aware that he was only a detective sergeant with not much in the way of prospects for getting higher than lieutenant or perhaps captain.

But she caught him up agreeably.

"It's fun for me to keep the place up. The apartment and Bernard are something besides work for me." She smiled at him and added, "When you have in people you like you want them to like it, too."

Then she made a little curtsy and said, "Susy's speech for the evening." She refilled his martini and listened to him as he turned to the case. At one point he interrupted himself.

"I wish I could talk about books or music sometimes, or something like that, but I don't know enough about them. The only other thing I know anything about is myself."

But she gave him no cue to begin on himself. He knew she recognized that this in turn would lead to her and to her marriage to Finnerton. And that disclosures about these would bind them closer than she apparently was ready for now.

The meal was simple and good. A cup of hot bouillon

with an egg yolk mixed in, tuna fish and sliced tomatoes, the first ones within reason that year, she told him, with chopped onions and olive oil dressing. They drank the wine with both the soup and salad and finished the bottle with the goulash and noodles.

She brought in a small fudge cake for dessert and he protested that he was too full for anything, but maybe one small bite.

"You brought in everything but the candlelight," he said to her over coffee. "It's going to be hard to get back to TV dinners and frozen pizza."

"No candlelight for first-time visitors," she said lightly. "Produces too many ideas. I don't want people to think I'm a mantrap."

Then she paused. The word "mantrap" had pulled them both up short.

In the sudden silence, Picard looked up at her, uncomfortable.

"Pulanske talked to me this afternoon, about what you mentioned out there in the graveyard, about being a decoy," she said quietly.

"What did he say?" Picard asked seriously.

Susy told him the homicide captain had pointed out that both women were probably picked up while street-walking near one of the half-dozen big downtown hotels, perhaps during a convention. Pulanske said that the odds were a decoy would not work, but that he, Pulanske, would be remiss if he did not use every device in the book to catch this man before he struck again. And, of course, Susy would get the best protection available. Captain Goldberg, from robbery, the finest stake-out man in the country, would help get the thing set up. . . .

"And so on and so on . . ." she said.

"So you're going to do it," he said solemnly.

"Yes, I guess so, Harry," she replied.

Well, thought Picard, Pulanske picked a good weekend. There were butter and egg men from some farm wholesalers' outfit at the Crowley-Shelton, and the gas and oil men at the Santa Lucia. There'd be plenty of big shots from the sticks, looking to cheat on the old lady. And the tony whores would be around to help them out.

"When's he want you to start?" he said aloud.

"Friday. Do you think there's any chance the man will show up, Harry, honestly?"

"Not much," Picard replied.

"Do you think it's worth while?" she asked.

"Yes," he said, "I guess so. If Pulanske didn't do it some jackass would be asking why he didn't."

"Well," she said resignedly, getting up and taking his coffee cup. "I'm no coward and no hero."

Picard looked at her. How nice, he thought, to say nobly, "Do not fear, Susy, I'll be there," but heroic words were not his forte.

She came back with a round fat bottle.

"This will leave a good orangy taste in your mouth, Sergeant," she said, smiling. He read the label: "Grand Marnier."

The conversation turned from the case to him, and he found it easy to tell her about himself. As he talked he looked at her, her hands at times cupping her chin, and the beginnings of the aging lines in her face. At thirty they are there, he thought, unconcerned about them. He told about the army, the abortive year in college, the first years on the force. How warm it was to be talking this way. She still shied away from talk of herself, but spoke freely, warmly of her boy, her brother's family in Detroit, the car, the apartment, all the things on the periphery of her life.

But relaxed now as their talk was, he knew he was on trial with her. She was quality stuff, perhaps too much so for him. He knew she liked him, might even let him make love to her. But he wanted more than that, and whatever she was, she was not going to be won by brashness.

He left at midnight. She helped him on with his topcoat, and then he turned and took her naturally in his arms. He kissed her carefully and thoroughly and thought he felt her melting toward him. But he let her draw back from his arms.

She studied his eyes for a moment, then hugged him. The door was open. Behind her was the warm apartment, empty except for the sleeping boy.

That was nice, he could feel her thinking. It was nice enough to make her want him to stay. But what he felt in her was not an invitation, just a statement of fact mixed perhaps with regret.

"It was a good way to spend an evening, Susy," he said, meeting her blue eyes one final time. But he knew that his best case lay in walking away and he did.

Next day, the Chapman House detective called early to tell Picard that, as he had suspected, the Scandian girl had come in only minutes before she called for the bellhop.

As he had with Sophie, Picard speculated, the killer had picked up the girl at a hotel, spent some time with her in whatever pursuit, then had driven her home for her to get a suitcase of clothes.

Fritz was busily compiling lists. One was a "hot list" of recent model black Dodges whose Washington plates had one of the professor's letters and a 9 on them. The other, broader list included all the dark colors, blue, maroon, green, and the blacks without the letters and 9.

The best prospects so far appeared to be cars registered to three men whose application addresses were motels or hotels from which they had since checked out. One of the men had an FBI record for embezzlement. The second had one arrest for disorderly conduct, another (no papered) for simple assault. On the third there was no record.

"I'll feel better when I nail down the third man, the guy who gave his address as the Shoreham, I mean the motel," Picard said to Pulanske. "We have mug shots on the other two and a fair file to work with. On this third guy, nothing.

"I'm going out to see what I can come up with on this Shoreham guy," he continued to Pulanske. "I've got the title. He bought that wagon three months ago at Mortie's Lot."

Pulanske walked toward the door with Picard. They were almost run over by Robley of General Assignment, a skinny gray-haired man who looked like a judge but was given to fantastic enthusiasm and fits of temper.

"We've got him, oh, oh, we've got him," Robley said to the two men, pushing at Pulanske's chest with some papers. The captain and Picard both instinctively drew back from Robley's assault.

"Oh Christ, ain't he a beauty," he said, holding a mug shot in Picard's face. "Listen," he continued hoarsely. " 'Matthew Mark Gustafson, 36, arrested Mobile, 1945, battery; Birmingham, 1947, housebreaking; Baltimore, 1955, attempted rape, acquitted; Washington, 1957, attempted rape, broken down to simple assault; Washington, 1958, assault with a dangerous weapon (knife).' "

Picard and Pulanske both looked over his shoulder as he read. Robley pointed his thin finger at each of the offenses, then flipped through the early statements of facts. They read intently the two statements on the Washington case of attempted rape and the knifing.

"God, that's lovely, Robbie. Where is the guy?" said Pulanske.

"I don't know, I don't know," sang Robley. "Maybe here at 7908 Eades Street, Southeast, that's the last address."

Pulanske was grinning, showing the big gaps between his incisors and canines.

"Harry, if you spot the car down there call me. Oh, call me anyway before you go to the house. We want to bring him back here for questioning, but we don't have enough for an arrest," Pulanske said.

"We can't lose this one on some screwball technicality about probable cause," he added. "I think you had better go by that bellhop with the mug shot first."

On the way out to the Chapman House, Picard's mind had already begun to play the devil's advocate. There was the accent. Well, maybe this guy was a Swede even if he was born in Alabama, Montevallo, Alabama. And his occupation was listed as mechanic. What was a mechanic doing in a chesterfield. Maybe a disguise.

The bellhop was inconclusive. He thought the man he saw had a longer face, but there was something the same about the nose. It was so dark.

Robley and Picard spent much of the afternoon talking with neighbors, without approaching the house. Yes, they said, that was the man they knew as Gus Markson—an alias used by Gustafson, the records showed. But they had not seen him around for some time, well, perhaps, two months.

When they finally rang the bell of the seedy two-story dwelling, they were reasonably sure the man would not be at home. But their hearts were beating heavily and both men had their right hands near the holsters they wore on their hips under their coats.

A woman answered. No, the man wasn't there. Yes, Markson, well, Gustafson then, had lived there. He was her common-law husband, if you want to call it that. No, she didn't know what he was doing now, said the weary-looking woman.

She'd heard the son of a bitch was doing time somewhere.

It was six o'clock when they found out from the Maryland Corrections Department that Gustafson had been safe in Maryland's Prison Camp Number Two for the last ninety days on a hundred-twenty-day sentence for drunk and serious disorderliness—a charge not picked up on the record from the FBI.

Picard was too disappointed to press on with the hunt for the automobile at Mortie's Lot. He went home and ate a TV dinner (turkey) while he watched the seven-o'clock news. Then he dozed for an hour before the alarm rang him awake to new chores.

He drove out to Susy's and got there about 9:30 p.m.

Mrs. Kearns, the baby-sitter, came to the door. A dumpy, florid woman, she always seemed out of breath.

The policewoman came out of her bedroom, dressed in an off-the-shoulder black dress. Except for her exaggerated make-up, she looked far too proper for a prostitute.

"I've borrowed a fur coat," she told Picard, looking at him guardedly. With a pursing of lips, Mrs. Kearns noted the excess of lipstick and mascara.

"Have a good time," the baby-sitter told them as they left.

Susy said outside that she had talked with Betsy after frightening the prostitute into a promise to keep quiet. Betsy had planned to be outside the Crowley-Shelton for the convention in any case and would have recognized her, Susy reasoned.

For oilmen, Betsy had confided, dress like a housewife. For the butter and egg men, make like a movie queen. Susy pulled out a pair of dark glasses as Picard started the car.

"Movie queen," she said, holding her chin up. Then she took them off and smiled at him, taking his hand.

"My God, Susy, you aren't going to find any Johns if you fix them with that blue stare of yours. All they'll think is how did the gal who married dear old Dad get mixed up in this."

She put the glasses down on the bridge of her nose.

"Better?" she said, poking his arm.

"Like a schoolmarm living it up. You could give an algebra lesson as a bonus to the first customer," he said.

"Very funny, sir," she replied, then more seriously, asked, "Where are you and the good Captain Goldberg going to be parked?"

Picard told her that he and the robbery-squad captain would be pulled into the driveway on the Sixteenth Street side of the hotel, about a hundred feet from where she would solicit. The hotel was informed that the two men were on a special but undisclosed surveillance. And the police in the Third Precinct had been told to leave the ladies alone that night.

For the first hour Picard and Goldberg watched closely as Susy paced slowly back and forth on the sidewalk beside the hotel, sometimes looking at her watch, occasionally talking to a lone man.

The robbery captain, after assuring himself that Picard was alert, flicked on a transistor radio he had brought with him, and dozed. Picard, although he found watching Susy pleasurable, soon tired of the unusual surveillance.

He looked for a tall man in a dark coat and a snap brim who would approach Susy or wander alone from under the big marquee of the hotel where a lighted banner saying "Welcome Dairy Wholesalers" flapped desultorily in the slight evening breeze.

Picard saw the girl Betsy arrive at the corner at about 11:30 p.m. But he had to look twice. She had dyed her platinum blond hair dark brown. The fact that all three victims had been blondes had not escaped the sorority of streetwalkers.

Betsy did not wait long. Two middle-aged men came up to her, talked a short time with her, and then went to the curb and stood uneasily together. She walked past them and into the hotel, and a few minutes later the two men followed.

Picard marked their passage. He envied them. He thought Betsy was a good-looking and pleasant whore.

The hours passed more slowly than he could have imagined. At 1 a.m. he roused Goldberg, who snapped from drowsiness to alertness. Picard fought sleep, then, exhausted, he began to doze. But he was uneasy. He dreamed he was walking into a blackness, was lost in a dark, deep fog. But before the dream could take that steep turn to terror, he awoke. Susy was looking into the car with her tired prostitute's face.

"Take me home, Harry," she said. "I'm bushed."

Picard slept late the next day. Then he drove out to the Shoreham motel, newly built behind the hotel. The man's name he was checking was Sebastian Paulier. The man had given this name and the Shoreham as his address when he bought the car three months before, and it was to the motel that the plates were mailed.

Although the manager was helpful, there was no name similar to Paulier on the registry, nor could the manager or any of the desk clerks on duty distinctly remember anyone of the suspected killer's general description.

"We have so many, so many," he kept apologizing. "And the Shoreham is the sort of place where people in good clothes with accents come."

The license tag application showed that the car was bought at Mortie's Lot near the old Gayety burlesque theater.

Mortie Roticella was one of the old-time used-car pirates whom even a hard-hitting newspaper series on bilkers had not been able to do away with. He began pretending outrage the moment Picard walked in. But the homicide detective was finally able to convince him that he was not under suspicion.

"Tell me, Sergeant Picard," said Mortie Roticella with feigned earnestness. "Tell me what I can do to help. Could this case be the big apple? I mean these babes in the river?"

Picard knew it was futile to lie to the auto dealer. But he coupled his acknowledgment that it was the "big apple" with a warning that the auto squad would come down hard on him if he gossiped.

"Well, I'm highly flattered, highly, by your visit, and very innocent, very innocent. I run a nice honest place since that goddamned newspaper tried to put us out of business—"

Picard cut him off. He showed him the photostats of the title, the tag application, and the registration.

"The guy may have been a tall man in dark clothes, he may have had an accent—" Picard started.

"Jesus, Sergeant, don't tell me any more about that son of a bitch," said the used-car man, glancing at the papers, then looking up. Picard felt his shoulder muscle contract with expectation. The used-car man stared at him, the concern showing as the folds of skin bunched around his eyes. Both knew they had hit something. And Picard, standing there in his topcoat, just as on any other day, on this light, blue-skied afternoon, felt himself being drawn close to something he both sought and feared.

"He had an accent?" asked the detective.

"Yes."

"He wore a chesterfield?"

"Yes, he had a snap-brim hat on, a black gangster job. He had a deep tan, but it didn't look real, it was more like that stuff you buy in a bottle to make you tan. It was too goldenish, you know."

Picard started to interrupt, but Roticella needed no encouragement. He spoke rapidly as if under a compulsion to rid his mind of a heavy burden.

"Nothing so awful happened if you just take it bit by bit, and you know I ain't no pansy, but somehow the whole incident, if I can call it that, scared the hell out of me.

"I was by myself here. It was one of them windy nights this winter, with the strings of lights blowing around, reflecting funny on the car finishes. But otherwise as black as spades. It was going on eleven, a Friday night when I stay open to catch the shines on payday.

"Well, there wasn't no shines that time of night and damned near nobody on the street with the damned wind whipping around. I'm diddling around with papers, and the door opens to the shack where I'm sitting with a big gust that blows the papers all over. So I look up to say, 'Jesus, shut the door,' but I don't get it all the way out.

"It wasn't that there was anything specially funny about this guy, part by part, except he smelled like he hadn't brushed his teeth for a year. I mean I could smell the son of a bitch all the way by the door. But here he comes so all of a sudden and the wind and I'm looking at these dead sort of eyes half closed and sort of fat red lips, in the sum total, you see, mean-looking.

"He sort of hisses, like he don't want to open his mouth, or has a wired-up jaw from being broken, or something. Anyway it's clear enough he's saying he wants the '61 Dodge out front and how much is it. I say I'm asking $3200, because he's lucky to find a black like that, which of course is a lie since nobody wants a black any more, they want pastels. Well, he looks at me angry like, and I figure it's not worth $2600 so I say, 'Because I need the money I'll let it go for $2900,' and he says $2800, so I shake my head and say well okay and start writing up the contract, talking about insurance and financing being a little extra.

"The next thing I know, he's counting off the hundreds from one of those king-sized wallets you carry in your inside coat pocket.

"Well, Sergeant, I just keep writing, and I ask, 'Name?' and he says Francis Andrews, and I ask, 'Address?' and he says 2500 Calvert, which later I find out is the Shoreham, but I'm busy writing now, I want to get the son of a bitch out of here.

"I ask him, 'Identification?' He don't say nothing, so I ask him again just like that.

"He says in his hiss, like a hoarse snake, that his license is at home and do I mind waiting for it. But I know damned well if that cash is hot and I've sold a car with no identification I'm in trouble with you guys. And trouble with the police I don't need. So I tell him, sir, any suitable identification at all will do. He says he hasn't got any and would I hurry up. Well, I don't like this guy's tone, Sergeant, and I'm thinking of the mickey I got in the desk drawer all ready and loaded for just such a damned case.

"I'm figuring now those hundreds might be hot, and for sure he ain't getting that car, not with my record, without no identification.

"So he up and grabs his money and is about to go out, but instead he turns around, and plunks it back on the desk. Now anybody else I would be throwing out of the office for this sort of crap. But this guy, I don't know why, gun in the desk and all, I don't want to monkey with him. Well, what does he pull out of his coat pocket, not a pistol by no means, but a Limey passport. He opens it up and there's a picture of him looking like Dracula with a sun tan, if you know what I mean. The name on it is all he lets me see, he holds it open for me on the desk while I write down Sebastian Paulier. Well, I see it ain't Francis Andrews, so I stop right in the middle of the name.

"I don't look up at him, but I say, 'Mister, that car ain't going out of here till tomorrow.' But he's ready for something like that because he shoots right back, 'Don't trifle with me. My work requires me to use a pseudername,' you know, a false name. Well, I truthfully don't feel like trifling with this guy, and then here is a passport on the up and up and the money, so hell, I sell him the Dodge.

"He takes the keys and the papers and the receipt I give him and he stalks away sort of like a cat, but somehow stiff-legged if you can imagine. Then off he goes in the goddamned Dodge.

"And, brother, that's the last I've seen and the last I ever want to see of that son of a bitch. I'll tell you, Sergeant, when I get home, I have myself a good solid belto before I go to bed to drive off the nightmares."

"You know that guy's driver's license should have been checked before you let go of that car, Mortie," said Picard quietly.

The used-car dealer bristled.

"Aw for chrissakes, Sergeant, you ain't gonna hold that against me after what I give you. I give you good dope on that damned guy, and don't kid me. . . ."

Roticella was right. It was "good dope." The hat, the coat, the sepulchral voice, even the strange walk and the accent. Picard fumbled excitedly for his cigarettes. This is my man, he murmured to himself. This strange man was the abductor of the women, the killer.

The homicide detective drove to headquarters. It was a quiet Saturday except in the big room across from the Chief of Detectives office where the "supersquad" was working.

On the way down the hall, the *Post* reporter called out and then caught up with him.

"How's it look, Harry?" said the reporter. "What was this gal doing at the Chapman House under an assumed name?"

"Frank, you'll have to dig that up yourself. I can't help you. No, nothing else too new. We'll let you know when we can."

Picard walked into the squad room, rapidly briefed the detectives on what he had learned from Roticella, and called Pulanske at home. "What do you think?" Pulanske threw back at him when he asked for instructions.

Picard said he feared a lookout on the car could bring publicity. The newspapers would pick up the lookout, their reporters would check back the plates to Paulier, and the fugitive would be warned.

"I think we ought to keep the number to ourselves until we can develop a little more on this bird," he suggested to Pulanske, and the captain agreed.

The tag number was TE 749. The professor had been right on only one letter and on the number, but this had been enough.

Picard asked Robley to work on alien registration and customs while he tried to get something from the British through their embassy.

The embassy was closed, but he telephoned the duty first secretary, who promised to help.

The duty first secretary was as good as his word. A vice-consul and security officer were waiting outside the old embassy building when he turned up Massachusetts Avenue and into the long driveway. In the vice-consul's office, the man offered Picard a seat, then went to a shelf in a closet.

"A spot of tea?" he asked, just as the British do in movies.

"Sure," said Picard, to the man's back. The vice-consul turned around bringing three glasses carried with his fingers in them and a bottle of scotch. He smiled cheerily with bad teeth.

"Tell us all, Sergeant," he said.

Picard told them there was some reason to think a Sebastian Paulier, about forty to fifty, about six feet, one hundred sixty pounds, carrying a British passport, number unknown, alias Francis Andrews, a resident of the U.S.

some three months, was a "hot" suspect in a murder. Yes, it was the Scandian one, but please keep it to themselves.

"I want to find out whatever you fellows can tell me about this Paulier," said the homicide sergeant. "I don't want to be melodramatic or anything, but he's about due again. Every two weeks he seems to be picking up some poor whore, or somebody he thinks is."

The two Britishers agreed to try.

"I don't think we can have anything before a couple of hours, do you, Wendell?" said the vice-consul to the security man. "Our Scotland Yard is still in the preautomation age on a lot of things," he added deprecatingly.

"What the bugger means is that he'll have some of those poor bastards over there kill themselves to have something over here in two hours, which he bloody well knows is twice as fast as your State or even your FBI could come back with," said the security man, Wendell Hugh-Matthews.

The vice-consul poured scotch all around again. Harry wished there had been some ice and water. He wondered if the banter was always this pleasant, that is, when an American was not present to appreciate it.

He returned to headquarters, feeling a little giddy from the "tea," and ate a hasty lunch with Pulanske, Robley, and Fritz. All four were nervous, knowing almost for certain that they had the right man, but unable to make it public, to begin the full-scale search. Robley asked Pulanske if he didn't think they could get a warrant on the man with what they had, but Pulanske shook his head.

"Him being a foreigner, that is, if that was really his own passport he showed Roticella, it's bad news two ways. On the warrant we got to have very hard facts, and he can use the damned passport to skip the country if he knows we're after him.

"Of course, if he does skip, we got him. There isn't

94

anybody would block extradition on a guy like that. Even the commies wouldn't have him."

The British were within their two hours by ten minutes. The security man reached Picard by telephone at the homicide squad.

The records were still being checked on the suspect, but this much was known so far. He came to England from Yugoslavia during that confused period right after the war just as the communist governments were taking over in one Balkan country after another.

He was admitted to Great Britain as an alien in 1945, as near as could be known, and was naturalized in 1950. The passport was issued a few months later, and was renewed through the British consul at Kuala Lumpur, Malaya. No, no idea in the world why he, or anyone for that matter, would leave England for Malaya.

On the personal side, the passport application showed that he was now forty-eight, unmarried at time of application. He said his occupation was farmer, but more likely he was the owner of an estate who feared trouble at the hands of the communists and was seeking a haven in England.

Next of kin was simply marked "deceased." And there was no one listed at all to notify "in case of . . ."

Height was six feet one inch, weight at the time one hundred fifty pounds, eyes brown, hair dark brown, complexion pale. The papers accompanying the nationality application were minimal. They showed that two Yugoslav doctors certified to his birthplace as a little town outside Belgrade. The official birth documents, as so many had been, were destroyed in Belgrade during the war. Various residences were noted in a half-dozen parts of lower-middle-class London, nothing exceptional for that time between 1945 and 1950. No known relatives in Great Britain. Education through the Gymnasium in Belgrade, a sort of European high school plus. First check of the files in Scotland Yard's central bureau showed no felony record at all. That was about it.

The security officer had anticipated Picard a bit and was asking for a report from the British consulate at Kuala Lumpur, plus whatever else London could produce from a check of his addresses and references. Picard was impressed, the more so because it was Saturday.

Robley's query to the FBI turned up that an S. Paulier had come into the country at Friendship International Airport, between Washington and Baltimore, on the night of December 20. His point of departure had been Quebec. The Department of Justice had no record of alien registration but was still looking.

The FBI would keep checking on the flight numbers and the people who talked with him at customs. The bureau also would see what could be learned from Canada.

The discovery of Paulier, or perhaps someone posing as him, as a pre-eminent suspect, shifted the functions of the supersquad.

Except for the single man working as a precaution on the other names and addresses turned up in the cross check of black Dodges, Pulanske concentrated the men on Paulier.

Had he come to Canada from Malaya? If so, what was his route, with whom did he talk on the way? The airline records could be traced back, but it would be tedious work. Customs officers, stewardesses, airline men must be questioned to see whether any clue to his present location had been inadvertently left.

Pulanske, as a matter of immediate importance, was asking the State Department to query the Malayan Embassy here and the U. S. Embassy in Kuala Lumpur. He was alerting Interpol to check its files. Above all, he wanted to establish speedily the man's *modus operandi*, his habits, his acquaintances, if any. The name of a single friend or a single peculiarity could point them to Paulier. The homicide captain believed that this routine could be carried out in the comparatively quiet way usual in such world-wide searches.

Pulanske hoped for a wire photo of the man's picture from London later in the day. It would be checked with the bellhop, with Betsy, with the professor, and with Roticella. Susy would also show it discreetly to prostitutes to see whether they had been encountered by the man.

Then, if Roticella and the bellhop could identify him with any assurance, Pulanske would seek a warrant.

Only when all else failed would Pulanske take the scattershot "Ten Most Wanted" approach. He preferred the manhunt to go on silently, outside the eye of the press and public, cleanly and classically until the man was arrested without fanfare.

Once the manhunt was on, Pulanske knew that his promotion was at stake. A failure to find Paulier would hurt him badly. The discovery that Paulier was the wrong man by some strange coincidence of events would finish his hopes, for there was no absolute assurance that the man they sought was not simply an eccentric but completely innocent European businessman here to sell tin and rubber and bearing a resemblance to an insane killer.

That night Susy took her walk beside the Crowley-Shelton again. Picard was already tired. Captain Goldberg, who set up the surveillance, was back with his own squad. Robley and Picard watched through the long evening as Susy walked to and fro, gradually adopting the slump-shouldered gait of the streetwalker—as characteristic and efficient in its way as that of a camel's long-suffering stride on the desert. He sent her home in a taxi, her vigil again futile, and drove with Robley to headquarters, where Pulanske and the supersquad were meeting at 2 a.m.

The little group around Pulanske were dog-tired to the man. Robley lay on the captain's couch, listening with his eyes half open and an arm with a cigarette in the hand dangling near the floor. Fritz, from the auto squad, watched Pulanske listlessly. The homicide captain sat on the edge of the desk, laying out the next day in a dull voice. In his hand he had an opened manila envelope. The British security man was sitting with him, looking as tired as the rest of them.

"This is Wendell Hugh-Matthews," said Pulanske to the detectives. "He's scared up an eight-by-ten of Paulier from his people in London, and it checks out with Roticella. No mistake." He nodded at Fritz.

"Roticella says no mistake," the auto squadman echoed. "We tried it on the bellhop and he says it looks like him, but he wouldn't want to swear to it unless we insist."

Hugh-Matthews looked mildly surprised as the Americans chuckled wearily. Pulanske pulled out the photograph, which was grainy but still clear.

"This is the boy," the captain said. "We are gonna get the affidavits from Roticella and the bellhop—on the car. And we'll need a sworn statement from the prof on the plate and the car, and that guy at Government Printing on the car at the bridge. Harry, I'll want a sworn statement from you on all the circumstantial stuff I missed, the prostitute, Betsy or whoever, and the motor vehicle stuff. I want a warrant on this by noon. We'll get Danny Young at the D.A.'s office to take it through the commissioner.

"Wendell," he said, turning to Hugh-Matthews, "could you swear us up an affidavit on the British records bit? It'd give the dossier some style." His voice sounded tired. "We'll shoot for accessory before the fact in the Scandian girl's murder," he said. "I just don't think we have enough for murder yet. We can always step it up.

"In this crazy jurisdiction," he said to Hugh-Matthews

again, "you got to have a warrant to arrest a jaywalker."

The warrant would be known only to the supersquad and the FBI. Pulanske did not want to send Paulier scurrying for cover with full-page pictures in the newspapers. But Picard—and Pulanske—knew well that with killers like this one publicity would mean only a brief respite from murder. His kinds of lust, Picard thought, are too great, too violent to be held back long by fear of discovery.

As they left the squad room, Fritz fell in beside Picard.

"Harry," he said, "something has just hit me about that picture, about Roticella." Picard turned to him.

"That passport picture," Fritz continued, "that picture of Paulier was taken thirteen years ago, but Roticella said it was the spitting image of how he looked that night on the lot. The guy hadn't changed a bit."

Picard said, "Thanks, Fritzie." At Paulier's age, he thought, at forty-eight, the years don't show much one way or the other. But the fact stuck in his mind, another isolated question mark in a strange case.

The next two days were an agony of frustration for Pulanske and Picard. A fruitless series of clues came in, from the mentally ill, from the malicious, from the misguided. Three men volunteered their guilt and confessed the three killings in great detail. But they were demented and, whatever they were guilty of, it was not the murders at hand. Futile running down of false leads kept the detectives nervous, irritated with each other.

Then a solid clue came in: the location of the customs man who handled Paulier at the airport.

The man's office, prodded by the FBI, found him on vacation in Yosemite. Picard reached him at the lodge and pressed him hard with a description of Paulier. But he drew a blank. Yes, the customs man said, he was on duty the night in question, the night the ticket showed, but he couldn't remember. Picard persuaded him to leave

Yosemite for San Francisco a day early. The detective sent a copy of Paulier's photograph by jet for the man to study at police headquarters in San Francisco. They spoke again by telephone, the man with the picture in his hand now while Picard sought to jog the customs agent's memory back over the months.

"This is an ugly duck all right," the man said. "I ought to remember a mug like that, but, boy, you're asking me to go back a lot of baggage."

"Look," Picard said, referring to his data from the airlines office in Quebec. "This guy had a lot of extra baggage, about a hundred fifty pounds' worth ... No, it doesn't say what kind it was, just the weight. It was a Viscount flight with twenty-three people on it. One of them was Congressman Burtley Casey of New Hampshire ... Oh, you don't know him? Well, try to think of that excess baggage, maybe a suitcase, a big trunk, European type trunk. The guy had a thick accent, cold-looking, deep voice ... No I'm not sure it was even baggage, it could have been golf bags—"

"Wait a minute, wait a minute," he heard the man on the other end of the telephone say excitedly. "I'm getting something. I'm getting something. There was a big trunk, a big black old-looking job with a brass hasp, the old kind with brass corners, yes, it does seem like there was some tall guy along with it."

Picard's hand sweated on the telephone where he gripped it.

"Now, here's the word on it," said the customs man. "Yes, it seems like a Canada connection. And if this is the fellow you're looking for, and I'm not saying it is, you understand, there was this big old-fashioned trunk along with whatever else he had, and there was damned little inside of it but it looked worn inside. I can see it right now.

"I said to him, 'That's big enough to set up housekeeping in, isn't it?' Yes, I remember very well ... No, I can't remember if he said anything back. I was just making conversation. Well, I remember it because we don't get much excess on the Canada flights, now you've jogged my memory. Sort of thing you'd have thought would have come on by ship. Why, it must have been five feet long, big enough for a man to get into if he scrunched up a little."

A check of Friendship Airport yielded nothing, no recollection by cab drivers or porters of a man on the way to Washington. And Quebec, after providing the useful airline information, could produce nothing.

Why Washington? Why not New York? Or Chicago? Picard wondered. These were big cities where a man on the run could get lost. Washington was small, much less absorbent.

"Maybe he figured all the foreigners here would make it a good place to lose his accent in," Pulanske reasoned. "We don't notice these distinguished-looking cats with accents the way they do other places."

Yes, thought Picard, and the foreigners don't hang together here the way they do in New York and Chicago. And then the big reason hit home. The bimbos aren't out on the street in New York—Washington's like London, and I guess everybody knows it, a sort of downtown Piccadilly every time there's a convention.

And missing prostitutes don't leave much trace anywhere.

Pulanske wondered when the killer would strike again, and whether he had left Washington. Perhaps he already had hit and the body was consigned to the river or to deep woods where no one had chanced. One thing continued to haunt them: their kind of killer would strike again and again until he was caught.

When Paulier struck again, it was discovered in an undramatic, even a commonplace way.

The tabloid *Daily News,* the city's liveliest and most irreverent newspaper, was tipped off by someone and reported that a "mysterious foreigner" was a major suspect.

The story brought a phone call to the supersquad from a Mrs. Pantelein, wife of a third-rate lawyer who had to all appearances fled her and two detestable children over a week before. The call was one of dozens that the story prompted, and less interesting than many.

The woman complained that she had tried in vain a week ago to interest the Missing Persons squad in the case. Now she had read of a "foreigner" in the *Daily News* and recalled that months ago her husband had spoken of closing a deal with a strange man with an accent.

A supersquadman was put on the lead.

Pantelein's partner told him that Pantelein, who did a little sleazy real estate business on the side, had left his office near Municipal Court one night ten days ago.

"He was discouraged," the partner said. "But then he was always discouraged." Pantelein, he said, talked that night of picking up a gift at a big department store—Hecht's—for his kid's birthday.

Now the partner had figured at first, when Pantelein didn't show up for work the next day, that he had left for a bender or to tie up with some bimbo in Atlantic City or someplace.

But Pantelein's wife had kept bugging him.

When he saw the story about the foreigner in the *News,* he had called the wife, and she too remembered that Pantelein had talked about a land deal with a funny foreigner some months ago.

The deal? Well, he remembered Pantelein saying the guy blew in one night when he was alone and about to shut the place up. He said the visitor spent half the time hissing and half the time talking in a voice like something out of a well, and wound up giving him three months' cash in advance without ever seeing the place.

The supersquadman took Pantelein's picture to the salespeople at Hecht's (no one remembered) and then to some of the smaller stores in the area. At the Sports Mart, a salesman remembered him as coming in—yes, about ten days ago—and he bought a complete baseball outfit for his kid. Yes, he did remember it for sure because the guy insisted on getting an Orioles insignia and he had finally rooted one out of the basement from last year; the store had ordered too few and they were already out of the first shipment this year. Paid for the whole thing by check.

A visit to the bank showed that the check was the last one to clear. If he had been on a spree, wouldn't he have written another check? the supersquadman reasoned.

The detective winnowed the lawyer's real estate deals from his ill-kept records. He carried the mass of papers to Picard, and the two of them began the laborious work of comparing the lawyer's leases with copies of Paulier's spidery European handwriting from the citizenship application, the passport, and the car purchase agreement.

Two-thirds of the way through the stack, on a $240 a month deal for a farmhouse out Rockville way, the signature "F. X. Peterson" jumped out at them.

"That's my baby," Picard said aloud, rising with excitement. The odd cursive script needed no handwriting expert to equate it with the Paulier handwriting.

"Oh God," said Picard tensely. "We're on our way."

Picard, Pulanske, Robley, and Fritz piled into the number-one homicide cruiser, and Fritz skillfully sped them through the early-afternoon traffic to the Rockville pike. At Rockville, the county seat, they picked up a county lieutenant to execute the warrant and in minutes were accelerating down the rural Gaithersburg highway.

Guided by the county man, they swerved off the main

highway and onto a potholed and narrow road near Derwood that led through scraggly trees that opened occasionally on newly green fields and weathered farm buildings.

The farmhouse they sought stood ramshackle and peeling on a hill. A muddy driveway cut off the road and ran a hundred fifty yards to the old frame house, a huge sag-roofed barn, and two outbuildings, all squatting aged and dull beneath the graying April sky.

Pulanske studied it a moment, then barked, "Pass it by," to Fritz as the car slowed by the turnout. "We need some more men for this one."

After a swift conference Pulanske decided to telephone for reinforcements—he did not want the police radio in the pressroom to give him away—and then stake out the farm to await evidence that Paulier was there.

Meanwhile, he dropped off Picard and Robley to question the two nearest neighbors, one of whom lived on a hillock less than a mile from the farm and commanded a view of the seemingly deserted old buildings.

Picard showed his badge to the suspicious woman in the neighboring farm and she quickly called her husband from the barn.

Yes, they said in answer to the detective's rapid questioning, somebody lived in the farmhouse. They knew because it had been vacant a long time and then, beginning a month or so ago, every night they'd seen car lights going up the driveway and stopping at the house. Then the lights went out. Mostly before dawn, when they'd got up early. The car stayed parked all day, a big black one.

Picard felt the sweat form under his arms. This would be the black Dodge, his quarry for so long—the car that had taken Sophie and the Heldwig girl and God knew who else to their fates.

They hadn't seen the car for several days, the woman said. Picard exhaled his breath sharply in frustration.

"Then how do you know he still lives there?"

"I saw the light go on and then off just before dawn today when I got up," said the old farmer. "I keep a half an eye on that place all the time, mister, with them funny comings and goings, and I ain't seen anybody leave today. I ain't ever even seen the man that lives there."

Picard thanked them and jogged down the lane to meet Pulanske and the others.

"Captain," he said, "a light went on there last night."

Pulanske brooded a moment. The stakeout, he decided, would become a raid. He did not want to risk Paulier's waiting out the day inside and then fleeing under cover of darkness.

Pulanske ordered the reinforcements arriving from Washington and Montgomery County to fan out in the woods stretching to the rear of the house. Four K-9 dogs were on the way from the city, and the traffic helicopter would stand by to aid any search or chase.

Pulanske's three aides, bulwarked by four FBI men and two Montgomery detectives, led the raiders. Their cars were soon assembled out of sight around a curve from the straggling farm. The plain-clothes men were armed with tear gas and shotguns as well as their side arms.

The first droplets of rain smacked the windshield as the lead car, driven by Fritz and carrying the Washington detectives, slipped into gear and lunged around the curve toward the turnoff.

"Here we go," Picard heard Pulanske growl as the homicide cruiser slowed, then skidded up the weed-choked driveway toward the barn. From the corner of his eye, Picard saw the FBI sedan turn smartly and accelerate up the stony drive.

Fritz roared straight toward the farmhouse, the car protesting and shaking in second gear. Picard gripped his detective special. Behind him Robley held a brutish sawed-off shotgun in both hands.

The cruiser, within feet of the wooden stoop, screeched as Fritz braked it hard. The four detectives bailed out into the farmyard, coughing from the curtain of dust raised despite the raindrops.

Already the FBI men in the second car, one with a ten-gauge riot gun, were sprinting hard toward the barn, their coats flapping against their legs.

Trapped! Picard thought with exhilaration. We've got the bastard in there trapped. And he's seen us coming and knows it.

The four Washington detectives threw themselves solidly against the clapboard of the farmhouse, wary of any shot from above. Picard shouted the prescribed litany of "Police, come out," which service of the warrant required.

There was no answer. The homicide sergeant, pistol in hand, stepped out quickly from the shelter of the house wall and tried the door. It was locked. He backed up and rushed forward at it with his shoulder.

Picard was a compact, tough man who prided himself on staying in shape. He gave the door all his strength through his shoulder. A hollow "clump" sounded as he struck it, but it failed to give. The huge impact bounced him back sprawling, his shoulder shocked with aching.

Then the big homicide captain rushed over and past him, smashed into the door with a heavy grunt. The door sprang open with a bang.

Picard, still panting with pain from his bruised shoulder, leaped up and rushed into the house behind the captain. A dank smell assailed him. The curtained windows and the gray sky outside closed the rooms in gloom. He saw no one.

Picard and Pulanske ran for the stairs. The sergeant reached them first. Hugging the wall, he scampered up them two at a time. At the top was a closed bedroom door.

He's there! Picard thought. He kicked the door near the

knob and it swung open. He lunged in a half crouch into the room. It stank of death. Pantelein, thought Picard.

But a quick glance showed him only an unmade double bed and black heavy cloth partially shutting off the windows. Picard threw the light switch and a single low-watt bulb cast its sallow light on the room. No one.

Pulanske kicked open the door to a second bedroom. It was empty, unlived in. The bathroom was neat except for a shattered mirror. It reminded Picard of something, and he dashed back into the bedroom, half crying in frustration at the escape of their quarry. The recollection was of a shattered mirror in the bedroom on a closet door. He flung open the door, his pistol ready, but again no one. Black pointed shoes were lined up inside, and a half-dozen black suits hung from the closet rod, but there was no Paulier.

Picard rushed to the window. It was locked. No escape there. Down below, he saw a uniformed man crouched near bushes to the right of the chicken house, looking up at the window, his watching eyes wild but attentive beneath the bald dome of his head.

Pulanske came out of the bathroom with a big handful of shirts and underclothes.

"Where are those goddam dogs?" he said to Picard, and did not wait for an answer, but rushed down the stairs.

The house was empty. Picard almost wept with disappointment. He had been so sure. And now their game had escaped.

Outside the rain was falling heavier. Pulanske snapped an order to a uniformed man who rushed off, to return a moment later with an electric megaphone from the homicide car.

The raiders, some now in rain slickers, others in drenched uniforms, collected swiftly in a circle of blue and brown and shiny black. There were forty or fifty.

"Men," he said hoarsely, "thanks for your help. I am

going to impose on you to search the woods and the farm-houses—occupied and unoccupied—until dark. Then you may go. Please be particularly careful as you leave the farm area to watch for slips of paper, cigarettes, anything of value. Please watch for turned earth that might be the burial place of the new victim.

"I want the ten men who raided the buildings to stay here for the time being," he added.

The wet policemen slogged off toward the woods behind the house. Pulanske and Picard walked briskly toward the barn. Picard looked up, hearing the whir of the helicopter, out of sight in the drizzly sky.

"Damn, damn," he muttered in general exasperation.

"Those damn dogs never came," Pulanske echoed.

The sagging barn creaked in the wind as they approached. It was getting on to dusk, and Picard could see the rays of flashlights through the open door. Robley, straw sticking to his cheap business suit, came to the door as they approached, then returned inside.

The barn was on two levels, the hay and machinery above, the deserted and fouled old cow stalls below. The door opened on the second level and they entered, smelling the odor of rotten decayed hay and a dead animal smell.

"Dead cat," Robley explained, pointing to a mass of hay from which a patch of mussed fur showed. The hay, in crude and loose bales, filled an entire side of the barn, tumbling down from the back wall in a weird crumbling pyramid.

Picard's heart jumped momentarily. Could the killer be in the mass of hay, panting, hiding in hopes that the police would leave. Not likely, for the uneven rampart of rotting bales looked unbroken, but still he wished the dogs were there.

Pulanske asked two of the FBI men—and told Robley—to stand guard on the hay. They would try to search it later.

Picard carefully descended a shaky staircase in a corner of the barn to its ground floor. The fresh tracks of the searchers were all over the mud that during the years had leaked through the crumbling masonry walls.

The eerie room of broken stalls and mud smelled dank, unused, noxious like the rest of the barn. From below, Picard could see a huge hole where the floor above had caved in at the center of the barn.

He could have put that body in the hay, Picard said to himself. It would be a change from the river, he thought grimly.

Where could Paulier have gone? Picard thought with irritation as he climbed back up the stairs. The detectives had found no footprints anywhere, but the raiders might easily have obliterated these.

Had Paulier escaped earlier, Picard wondered, gone to his car, parked somewhere in the neighborhood, and driven away, perhaps forever, while they roared up the driveway and madly searched the house?

But Picard had no time for musing now. He hustled up the remaining steps and out of the barn. Like a dog on a scent, he stopped first at the chicken house, slipped and fell, then got up and peered inside. He was looking for clues. But the cheap lath and pine-wood hut held only old, damp feathers and chicken droppings.

Pulling his slicker tighter around him, he walked through the wet farmyard to the utility shed. His nerves were on edge and he reached for his pistol as the door opened, then relaxed as he saw it was Pulanske. The big homicide captain carried a rusty hayfork and a shovel, its handle broken short.

"Gotta start on that hay," grumbled Pulanske, his gruffness only partially hiding his disappointment.

"Be down soon," Picard answered, entering the equipment shed. But there, too, there was nothing of value: an ancient harrow, the skeletons of other old farm tools, a stack of soggy burlap bags that he viciously kicked apart—finding nothing.

He walked briskly toward the house, still hopeful for a fresh spoor that could gear them into the action of a search. But the cloudy twilight had turned toward darkness. He snatched his flashlight from the holder in the homicide car and circled the house. There was a mound of ashes near the back door. He shot the beam of light into the sodden ash pile and what looked like a pearl glistened. He reached into the ashes and pulled out a shirt button, charred but whole. Fishing further in the mess, he found a piece of fabric. Picard took his finds into the house.

An FBI man in the kitchen looked up from where he knelt by the ash door of the big potbellied stove.

"Buttons?" he asked when Picard held out the little object.

"Yep," said the detective.

"Me too," the FBI man said. He shoved Picard a piece of paper with several more buttons and two pieces of blackened fabric on it.

"Maybe he burned his shirts instead of washing them, or maybe he burned the clothes of the people he killed, God knows," the FBI agent speculated.

A sudden shiver came over Picard. What was that other unanswered question that throughout the frantic search had pricked the back of his mind? The mirrors, of course.

"Why the hell did he break the mirrors upstairs?" he asked himself out loud. The FBI man looked at him curiously. Picard turned and ran up the stairs.

The mirror in the bathroom was shattered and then knocked from its frame. Tiny slivers still hid in crevices of the old linoleum floor. In the bedroom, the long mirror on the outside of the closet door, an obviously anomalous adornment to the old farmhouse, had also been shattered.

Picard thought of the picture of Paulier—the full lips, too red, the cold, lifeless stare, and the lank, brownish-looking hair. A face utterly without warmth or humanity.

Why would he want a mirror with a face like that? thought the detective, half affrighted by the loneliness of the upstairs in the old creaking house—and the inhuman vision he had summoned up.

And there, in the closet, the suits and shoes: all neatly lined up, all ready for a strange man from God knew where to don them and go out to kill, viciously, from an unknown lust.

A deranged killer, Picard thought, who hated himself so he could not look in a mirror. The detective returned to the bathroom and opened the linen-closet door. Towels, sheets, washcloths, pretty much like . . .

"Hup," he said involuntarily. What was this? Two half-filled Man-Tan bottles. On the floor of the closet, pushed back, a dozen empties, a graveyard of the rectangular bottles that had held artificial sun-tan lotion.

Picard's mind snapped shut on Roticella's words: ". . . like Dracula with a sun tan." That is what the used-car man said. And here was the sun tan. He poked among the bottles on the floor. A rubbish of dentifrice cans, toothpaste tubes, toothbrushes. He pulled out one of the toothbrushes. Its bristles were worn almost flat.

Again a thrill of terrible recognition went through him. The breath—Roticella had said the man's breath was foul—and here was the killer's attempt to hide it.

Picard started downstairs, but an FBI man met him coming up the stairs.

Picard's mind was still seeking somehow to square his bewildering findings, but automatically he asked the agent what he'd found.

Well-used ironing board, pressing cloth, shoeshine kits—two—said the agent. "A real neat guy," he added.

"Oh yes, a Hermes portable. Didn't some kind of note come from Baltimore on a Hermes?" said the agent.

"Yes, yes," Picard stuttered. "The note with the money for the girl's burial. On a Hermes. Anything else?"

"Funny thing, no food in the house. Guy must've ate out—"

"What?" Picard gasped. The thin bodies of the two women passed his mind like ghosts. "No food?"

"Harry, what's the matter with you?" said the agent, taking his arm on the stairway and giving him a shake. "You hit that door too hard?"

Picard collected himself. The discoveries had come too fast. He felt tense, almost dizzy, but assured the FBI man that he was all right and continued down the stairs.

He walked carefully through the living room. A floor board was torn up where one of the raiders had checked for clues—or Pantelein's body, or Paulier—between the floor and the earth beneath. Now, like busy ants, the identification men had begun dusting.

Picard opened the door to seek Pulanske. A gust of rain blew out of the darkness and into his face. He buttoned his slicker. Night was on the farm, but the light of a car in the farmyard shone on a little group of men and an animal— the K-9 station wagon had come.

Picard slopped through the thick mud toward the group. The dogs would be thwarted by the mud, he feared.

Pulanske was talking to the handlers. They had been kept overlong on a double rape case. Pulanske was arguing that his case had priority over everything, but the handlers, short-tempered now, kept saying, "We got our orders."

The big German shepherds, each with his uniformed handler, filed up through the mud toward the house, led by Pulanske's burly form. The last dog, a bloodhound, contrasted sharply with the smart-looking police dogs. A man in an old field jacket and the trousers of an Occoquan workhouse guard led the sad-looking young bloodhound on a leash. The sag-faced dog's tongue lolled out, making its caricature of a face still more ludicrous.

Picard fell into step with the man.

"Good dog?" he asked, making talk to ease his own tension.

"Yes, suh," said the guard in the soft accents of Virginia, but there was a distant formality in his words that discouraged further talk.

At the front stoop of the house, an FBI man came out with the shirts and underwear Pulanske had found earlier, and a pair of Paulier's sharp-toed black shoes. The agent squatted in the doorway, holding the clothes out toward the dogs. Picard watched closely.

The first dog left the semicircle of men and his master led him to the garments. The dog approached with his nose out-thrust, but suddenly, sniffing the garment from a few inches away, recoiled violently, flipping his master in the mud and cowering at the far end of the leash from the clothes.

Picard laughed involuntarily, then caught himself and watched the strange behavior nervously. The dog cringed as the officer arose and shouted at him. He gripped the dog's collar and urged his nose into the clothes. The FBI man poked them out farther from the shelter of the stoop porch, but the dog, whining, pressed backward, bucking to shake free of his master's grip. The uniformed man, his raincoat running mud, walked him away, talking to him harshly in exasperation.

The two other police dogs refused the proffered clothes, shaking their heads vigorously as if to wriggle out of the restraining collar and cringing from the garments.

Picard, deeply unsettled by the performance, turned to Pulanske, but before he could question, the captain shook his head in bewilderment, pressing his lips tightly together.

The city-workhouse guard, a bedraggled figure among the neater officers, approached the clothes cautiously with his bloodhound's leash knotted across his knuckles. The big brown dog did not panic as the others did, but after a single sniff rubbed his sensitive nose in the mud. The guard did not press him, but led him back out through the ring of men. Picard could hear the bloodhound sneezing and snuffing with disgust.

"C'mon, Harry," said Pulanske, "we got to try to dope this out."

The two men went inside the house, and Picard, without seeking to speculate, laid out for the captain the bizarre findings: the mirrors, the sun-tan coloring, the toothbrushes . . .

Pulanske was obviously weary. He put his big head in his hands, then looked up blankly at the identification men, who busily worked at their specialty, ignoring the other officers.

"I don't know . . ." he began, but they were both started from their chairs by an unearthly sound outside.

They rushed to the door and peered into the rain. Officers were gathered around the bloodhound in front of the house. The dog, uttering half barks, half groans that seemed too human for a dog, too animal for a man, was once more near the clothes. Emory, the dog's master, squatted beside him with the clothes in his hand.

The Virginian, a skinny man with a day's beard, was talking gently to the dog in the center of a circle of detectives.

"You ain't gonna let me down now, Buster boy," he said to the nervous hound. "You gonna find that fellow, just like I taught you to, Buster boy. Now I want you to sniff this shoe. Yessir, yessir, now just one little sniff."

Emory held the shoe about a foot from the dog's nose and patted his head.

The rain was lighter, now, but still steady. "How the hell can he do anything in this mud?" said Picard to Pulanske.

The dog let out another of the hoarse bark-moans, but did not pull away from his master. The man put the black Oxford shoe, damp and spattered with mud, on the ground.

"Buster boy," said the Virginian softly, "let's give it just one little sniff, Buster, just enough for you to know all about it, all about it." He looked soothingly at the dog, then at the shoe, and to Picard's surprise went down on all fours and sniffed the shoe with his small, running nose.

The dog hesitantly stretched his neck, thrusting his nose suspiciously toward the shoe. He sniffed near it. A deep growl, so far back in its throat that it almost seemed to come from outside the dog, brought the circle of men to tense watchfulness. The bloodhound growled loudly now and turned and snapped at the air nearest one of the Montgomery detectives.

"Jesus," the man said, jumping backward.

"You have it, you have it, don't you, Buster boy?" said the Virginian with urgent encouragement. He scrambled to his feet.

The dog, who when he arrived had exhibited the resigned but doubtful gloom of all bloodhounds, was now fiercely snapping the air, pulling at the leash, which the Virginian had doubled around his wrist.

"God, I never saw a damned bloodhound act like that," said Pulanske. He and the other detectives moved back. The leashed bloodhound jerked his master through the group of men and out of the circle of light.

The dog coursed about the farmyard, growling and barking hoarsely as he sniffed the ground, trying desperately for a solid scent. A half-dozen of the raiders with flashlights followed the Occoquan dogman. The lights played eerily across the man's bending and twisting back and on the big brown dog in front of him. The men's quiet cursing as they slipped and stumbled in the mud and darkness blended with the voice of the bloodhound.

The dog crisscrossed the front yard, then headed in a long circle around the side of the house. At the back door he gave a screaming bark that he cut short suddenly. He's got the scent! Picard thought excitedly. Then he bayed one time with a voice that shook Picard with its otherworldness, the essence of all the dog sadness ever known. Sniffing intensely now, the bloodhound made for the barn, which loomed as a huge dark hulk in the rainy night. The flashlights flicked across the barn's wet, weathered sides. Pulanske growled at his men.

"Harry, Robley, McConnell, and Jonesy with me. You others fan around the building, and get those two uniformed men up by the house, quick, quickly."

As Fritz left, Pulanske grabbed his arm and hissed to him to get the Coleman lantern from the homicide car trunk. He handed the key to Fritz, who disappeared in the rain.

The detectives rushed after the Occoquan man, who was being dragged by the bloodhound toward the barn.

A Montgomery detective who had been working at the bales inside appeared in the barn doorway and the flashlights blinded him for a moment. Picard was surprised to find his own hand again going toward his pistol as he saw the detective. God-damned edgy, he thought, for he had known that the man would come to the doorway when he heard them approach.

The dog and its master and Pulanske rushed into the barn, and Pulanske threw the floodlight beam of his lantern on the rotting hay and the caved-in section of flooring.

"Watch that damned floor," he shouted to the guard, but the Occoquan man had already drawn back, dropping the leash as he did so. The brown dog bounded around the old sagging planks in the center to the musty bales at the far end of the cavernous barn. Pulanske and the others tracked the big-shouldered animal with their lights as he rushed up to the hay. The bloodhound bit at it twice, then retreated about four feet, barking hoarsely. He feinted toward the pile but was unwilling to approach it again.

"Paulier, Paulier," shouted Pulanske at the pile over the wild barks of the dog. "Come out. Come out. We are armed and have you surrounded. Raise your arms and come out."

The other detectives flashed their lights on various parts of the immense rotten heap, lighting all of it well enough for them to see any shifting of the lopsided bales that would alert them that a man was emerging.

"I don't believe he's in there, Chief," said the man from Occoquan. "If he was, Buster'd go on up to it. I don't know what he's got in there, though. I ain't never seen him this way."

The homicide captain lowered his gun. Behind him Fritz got the Coleman lantern going with a sizzling sound and its garish purple light, coming with a sudden glare, brought uneasy curses of surprise from the detectives. In a moment it was adjusted. Fritz hung it from a nail in the wall, from which it threw ghastly light and shadows through the vast old structure.

Emory skirted the rotten center flooring and recovered the leash. Softly he began talking to the dog. The barks turned first to a deep growl, then to a whine of anxiety.

"Calm down, Buster boy, calm down, baby boy," the Virginian continued.

Pulanske was indecisive for a moment.

"I'd like to work that pile over with a couple of tommy guns and some tear gas," he growled half to himself. But Picard knew that the homicide captain was not that kind of operator. He would first try to bring back his man alive. He would kill only when his own life or the life of one of his men was in danger. This was Pulanske's professional way.

"Will," he said to the big FBI man who had begun the raid with the riot gun. "Get that cannon of yours. I want you to stand by while we dig out whatever is in that damned hay." The FBI man left and was back in moments. Pulanske turned to the Occoquan man.

"Emory, can that dog tell us what part of the pile worries him?" The Virginian shook his head and replied without raising his voice, "Buster has about done what he'll do tonight. He'll just get upset if I try to put him up against that pile of fodder again. He may be ruint now with all this going on, whatever it was in there."

The men outside had ascertained that there was no crack in the walls behind the hay big enough to allow a man to escape. Pulanske nonetheless had two of the police cars driven skidding and grinding into the mud to where they could train their headlights on the hay side of the barn.

On the lower level, below the hay, the floor sagged downward, but there were no loose-looking boards. Pulanske left one of the FBI men and a county officer below with an electric torch as a precaution.

Upstairs, the jagged incline of the bales created a shadowy mountainscape where it was projected against the barn's wall.

The detectives worked at the bales with their arms, the broken shovel, and the old hayfork. Their shadows, magnified into giants by the lantern projection, labored grotesquely above them.

One of the laborers had extricated the dead cat earlier and thrown it out the door, but the odor of corruption lingered.

"Could that have been what he smelled?" Pulanske said, interrupting his labors to turn to Emory.

"No, Chief, that dog knows dead cats." The Virginian led the dog outside to where the cat's body lay in the rain. Picard watched the dog, tense and silent now, sniff the body, then turn away without reaction.

"See," said Emory simply.

The rain, carried by the wind, beat the tin roof in waves and dripped through in a half-dozen places. The sweating men worked on.

The floor was soon covered with sodden bales. The policemen began throwing them through the hole in the floor, which led downward to the old stalls. There, below, the FBI agent and the county officer sat in chairs borrowed from the house. Bundled in their coats, they watched drowsily as one bale after another dropped down to their level.

Picard was weary. The rage that had filled him when he first broke down the door had turned first to acute exasperation, then to frustration at the mystifying clues, and now to an edgy sense of ill ease. The fantastic behavior of the dogs was one more cause for his uneasiness.

He heard a heavy clump as one of the uniformed men working at the side of the pile pried a tower of bales forward with a hayfork brought by the county reinforcements. Then the officer jabbed deep behind the stack with his fork.

"Hunh!" he shouted. The men stopped work and heard a hollow "boom" as the man struck something hidden behind remaining bales next to the wall.

"Come out!" Pulanske shouted at the worker, a newly arrived county officer, and the man jumped over the fallen bales and emerged covered with hay.

"There's something hollow back there, solid though, I hit it with my fork," the man gasped.

Pulanske drew his revolver and clicked off his safety. Two of the FBI men took back their forks from their reliefs. Robley picked up the riot gun, handed it unconsciously to the big FBI man, and went to work with a third fork. They labored silently but fast—the new arrivals stepped back, ringing the workers with concerned faces. As they moved the damp bales, two of the ID men crept into the barn and watched the tense semicircle.

One of the FBI men struck the object, and again it gave off its heavy resonant thud. His fork uncovered a corner bound in brass, then more of it, and Picard saw that it was a big steamer trunk lying on its side.

"That's it," Picard hissed to Pulanske. "It's the thing the customs guy was talking about." The FBI men gingerly speared and thrust aside two more bales, uncovering the entire lid of the trunk. Pulanske holstered his pistol, stepped between the two FBI men, and took the fork from one of them. With its handle he gave it a rap. It resounded hollowly.

Robley and two other detectives stood by with pistols drawn while Pulanske and the FBI man finished uncovering the trunk. Will lowered his riot gun. The range was too close and his comrades were too tightly bunched for him to use it.

The trunk stood clear of the hay. Pulanske shoved it hard with his foot. It moved against the pile. Then he reached under it and turned it on end.

"Nothing," he grunted. "It's empty."

Pulanske tried the lock, but it refused to open. Robley, the general-assignment squadman, went to his cruiser for a crowbar. He forced the lock easily, and Pulanske sprang the side hasps open and flung back the lid.

Picard was near enough to catch the smell from the trunk full in his nostrils. It was a smell neither fecal nor ammoniac. It was the smell of the dead unburied, the corrupt smell of the unclean abattoir, of the charnel house. He had smelled it before only in the rooms of those who died and lay dead behind locked doors until their decomposition brought discoverers.

Picard moved forward, patting around the worn inside of the trunk. In two places there appeared to be blood streaks, neither new, and in other parts of the finished cotton fabric there were light places as if spot remover had been used liberally. On the bottom of the trunk, he felt a little give and folded back a heavy canvas shield that had been stretched with a fastener. Beneath it was dry dirt, a layer of dry earth bunched near one end apparently from the kicking and shifting the trunk had undergone.

Picard picked up some of it, then dropped it back in the trunk.

"Dirt," he said to Pulanske, who looked stunned at the discovery. "Just plain dry dirt hidden purposely under that canvas."

The detectives gathered around, looking at the earth, then turning their heads away from the smell of the trunk.

"The stink?" Pulanske asked himself out loud. "Maybe he carted that poor damned lawyer around in this thing, or one of the girls, or God knows who. There's the blood . . ."

But the killer had disposed of the bodies of Norma Heldwig and Sophie before decomposition began, thought Picard.

The homicide captain knew that there would be no return of the killer, but he positioned his men as if it were a probability.

Picard and Will Jones, the FBI man, would take the first shift in the barn. Three others would stand by inside the house, and for short one-hour tricks the uniformed men would stand outside the barn and the house. Pulanske planned to doze if he could in the house and he advised those not on duty to do the same.

Picard and Jones settled into chairs brought from the house, and the other detectives dispersed. The captain himself stayed behind briefly in the chilly, empty barn. He walked toward the open trunk, its brass corners shining in the glare of the Coleman lantern.

"Any ideas?" he asked, turning to Picard.

"No," said Picard in a tired monotone. Then he mused. "Oh, I don't know, I guess there's ideas. Just no answers. We can figure this is the trunk he brought with him from wherever he came from. But with a stink like that it would never have gotten by customs without the customs man remembering. So either the stink wasn't ever in it, or at least it wasn't this bad when it passed customs.

"That smell, that odor, Captain, isn't just like death by itself, you know that. I can't help remembering what Roticella said about how this guy's breath smelled, like he hadn't brushed his teeth for a long time, is the way he put it.

"The easy way to look at it would be that the trunk smell is from one of his victims. I mean that's the natural thing and it takes care of the blood on the fabric and the cleaned spots. But Paulier, this guy, has never waited, at least in the two cases we know about, for rot to set in. He's shucked off his victims fast. And would he have brought this trunk all the way from Europe, say, just to hide bodies in? Mustn't he have some reason for bringing this trunk all that way?"

Pulanske smiled wearily. "I don't know, Harry, you tell me. You're turning into a criminologist in front of my eyes."

Picard stopped and lit a cigarette. He felt that he had let himself run to speculation without facts to back it up.

"Maybe so," he said, "maybe so. Maybe he couldn't chuck Pantelein as fast as the others. Maybe he used the trunk overseas to hide people he killed and just got used to it."

The homicide captain was watching him closely.

"Or maybe what were you going to say before?"

Picard drew deeply on the cigarette.

"Maybe he hid himself in that trunk for some reason," he said quietly, "some screwy reason we can't even imagine."

"Hid from what?" asked Pulanske, surprised.

Picard shrugged.

The FBI man, who had been silent, interrupted.

"Harry, he was sleeping in the bed in the house. The bed upstairs was slept in, I checked it. Why the hell would anybody hide in a trunk when they got a bed?"

Pulanske joined in.

"And the dirt. How does the dirt in the trunk figure?"

Picard felt hemmed in. The unmade bed? Of course it was logical that Paulier slept there rather than in a cramped trunk. The dirt? He had no answer for that, none at all.

"Maybe the great and glorious FBI lab can tell us where the dirt came from," he said, half jest, half sarcasm.

Jones drew back his arm in mock assault.

"I'm not knocking your idea, Harry," said the agent. "You know, that trunk wasn't wedged in there solid. There was room enough between the wall and the hay for a skinny man to squeeze up to it, maybe even for the damned lid to open. It was just a couple of bales blocking the way to it. But hell, man, nobody sleeps in trunks."

Pulanske was skeptical too. The passage could easily have been a result of Paulier's burrowing to hide the trunk when he moved it to the barn, and unused since then.

Picard feared that he was right. The obvious was so often the true. And certainly the obvious was that the trunk was either simply stored—hidden—by Paulier, or used as a temporary coffin for his hapless victims.

The homicide captain walked out of the barn. The rain had softened to a drizzle, but the yard in front of the farmhouse was awash with muddy water. The purple glare of the lantern shining through the open door sent a huge avenue of light running out onto the wet yard. The FBI man and Picard watched as Pulanske heavily picked his way to the house, then they closed the barn door and returned to their chairs.

After a few minutes, the door creaked open, and the FBI man was flat against the wall with his gun out almost before Picard could leave his chair.

It was the Virginia dogman and the big bloodhound.

The FBI man looked at Picard with embarrassment, then decided it was best to laugh off his obvious conditioning.

"Clean living, Harry," he said.

Picard smiled weakly. The trouble with the FBI, he thought glumly, was not that they seemed good, but that they were good.

The Occoquan guard came over to where they were sitting and plumped down on the floor. He opened a paper sack and offered them each a baloney sandwich, brought in by the Metropolitan uniformed men who had come to relieve the county police.

"They got them at the cell block," said the guard apologetically.

"Any coffee?" asked Picard.

"No," the workhouse guard said. "They didn't have no time."

The three men chewed on the dry-tasting bread and meat. Emory squatted in front of the dog and patted him, giving him half of his sandwich. The young bloodhound ate it solemnly.

"You really love that dog," remarked Picard.

"Yes, he's a good dog," said the man. "It takes doing to train a dog like this. But when you finish you got something that beats people for friendship." Then he realized that he had said more than he wanted, and went back to his sandwich and his charge.

"How come the German shepherds shied away?" said the FBI man. "They scared or something?"

"I reckon," said the dogman. "They knows what they don't want and they leaves it alone."

"Then how come Buster didn't leave it alone?" persisted Jones.

"He's gotten like me, he's a damned fool. He hasn't got enough sense to stay away from what don't concern him like them Germans," said the Virginian gloomily.

"What was there to stay away from?" said Jones, unwilling to let the subject go.

"You know better than me, Mr. FBI," the Occoquan guard replied with rude finality. "You guess what it was."

Picard got up from his chair and walked to the trunk. The fabric inside was not uniformly worn, but worn only in spots where it appeared to have been frequently rubbed. He picked out a few lumps of earth and crumbled them in his fingers.

He stretched the canvas back over the bed of earth, fastened it, and then closed the heavy lid of the trunk. He latched the end hasps but made no effort to hammer shut the sprung lock. Big as a coffin, he thought.

The trunk's odor still clung on the moist air of the barn. The barn seemed vast, cold, and lonely with the rain no longer beating its roof. Far away, outside, he heard a dog's bark.

The homicide detective returned to his chair. The Virginian was lying along the wall, the dog near him, looking from his sad eyes outward at nothing.

From Picard's chair the trunk, fifteen feet away, looked like a coffin at a wake. The Coleman lamp left the three men in the shadows, but the trunk stood out, the silent center of every eye that came to the barn.

★

The minutes passed by, so long that Picard seemed aware of every one of their sixty seconds. Surely the man was gone now, he thought. To Los Angeles, or out of the country with his British passport. The old barn creaked as a night breeze blew up outside. The scrape of the tin roof against its wooden supports gave a strange, regular counterpoint to the squeak of the walls, wood against wood.

Picard was drowsy from waiting. He thought disconnectedly of the case. Where was Paulier now? Where was Susy? It was Friday night. The rain would save her from streetwalking. He thought of her swing as she walked, as he watched and dreamed warmly of a bed and Susy. He forced his mind away. No time for that.

Where was Pantelein, where was he? Where were the others the madman killed? Picard thought with a shudder of the Scandian girl. Ten days, twelve days ago. The father had left the country yesterday, or the day before. He had taken her ashes back to Scandia. In a Swedish glass urn, no doubt, thought Picard with mild disgust at the niceties with which the prim cloak the repulsive fact of death.

Who was the first victim? Would they ever know? Probably not. Picard's mind stirred to the possibility that Paulier was holed up with some British or Yugoslav or even Malayan acquaintance. But there was no criminal element as such among any of these nationalities in this country. Why had the man come to this country anyway? The land of opportunity, he thought grimly. Then seriously, That's easy. Where better to get lost? No papers needed for hotels, no documents to be carried at all times. Another foreigner in a country of foreigners, a city of foreigners. Lost in the swarm.

He glanced at his watch. An hour of the two-hour trick to go. Why couldn't the uniformed men do this? he thought bitterly. No, Pulanske took no chances on a screw-up even if it ruined his detectives' health. He looked at the FBI man. Jones was staring at the trunk through glazed, half-closed eyes. But he had already seen how fast the FBI man could move.

The Virginian was sleeping, his hands on his legs twitching as his body relaxed. The bloodhound seemed to sleep too, snorting quietly or whimpering momentarily as dog dreams no man could know tore through his ugly head.

The cold made a tooth Picard had meant to have filled throb uncomfortably. The old barn sighed and groaned with the wind.

What was Paulier thinking now? he wondered.

Did he fear death or capture? What did he fear? What thoughts go through a mind that is sick like his? Picard thought of Norma Heldwig's hideously slashed throat. Are they even human thoughts, or more the thoughts of a wolf? Are they wolf desires that are under control, but become too strong, too animal to contain, that break out into the rage of madness that had caused these dreadful killings? But they are more than wolf thoughts, Picard mused. Paulier had been able to combine his madness with huge intelligence and cunning to avoid them, the detectives seeking him, to avoid giving the definitive clue that would lead like an arrow to him in his lair.

Where was his car? Picard wondered. The car that he, Picard, loved so because it was this that gave him the first clue to the murderer's name, the black and lovely Dodge clue. How did he escape? Did he kill Pantelein right away? Maybe. Maybe not. What happened to his victims between the time they disappeared and the time they died? Did he starve them? Lock them away to watch them die? Something horrible, weird? Drink their blood? Ugh, thought Picard. Or did he practice some obscene intercourse, as in that British case? Not apparently with the Scandian girl. Why did he pick Pantelein, a man? Girls too risky? To shut him up?

Did he question the lawyer to find out whether he had put the police on his trail?

Ah, the crafty, lousy lawyer Pantelein. Picard could hear him assuring the killer:

"To be sure, mister—er—I don't recall your name, you can trust me without a qualm, without a qualm, oh, you will never, never be troubled."

Or had Pantelein even recognized the man who whisked him off to death. Or how wild if Paulier had nothing to do with Pantelein's disappearance, if the lawyer even now were laughing, making love to his bimbo in Miami, New York. After all, they found no evidence at the farm to establish Pantelein's presence there.

Picard thought of all the crooked attorneys he knew in his own homicide cases who for a fat fee had bribed or tricked or threatened government witnesses to disappear, to commit perjury. Ah, the legal canons. Pantelein was their sacrificial goat perhaps, Picard mused.

Picard jerked his mind back to the case—the saliva on the Kleenex, the dirt, the mirrors, the loss of weight—but again it wandered off wearily.

He, Picard, would be glad for dawn. He would go back to his apartment and would sleep. Yes, the others could search the farm for the grave of Pantelein, Esq., attorney-at-law. Picard would sleep.

His head dropped down, awakening him from his half sleep.

The trunk was before him in a pool of light. A magic box, black and shiny with brass studs and corners and fasteners glowing warmly. Picard, lulled by the regular sounds of the creaking barn, dozed; he was driving back to his apartment, yes, back to the bed, to sleep . . .

The harsh, short barks of the bloodhound snapped him

awake. His first thought was that the dog had a nightmare. He could not locate himself for a moment and fumbled for his pistol.

The FBI man was not so quick this time, but both men had their pistols and flashlights out before the Virginian came up from his cold bed by the wall. The bloodhound cringed next to his master, growling deep back in his throat now, but softly.

The two law-enforcement men fidgeted. The Occoquan guard patted the dog, trying to calm him and still only half awake.

Picard had just begun to relax when the dog began to bark wildly, his body squirming to and fro in an effort to get away from his master and closer to the wall. Picard looked to the opposite side of the barn where he felt the dog sensed a presence.

There were quick footsteps.

The detective jumped up, but not in time to see who it was that dashed the lantern to the floor, where—its delicate mantle dissipated—it hissed futilely.

He flicked his light toward the broken lantern, crouching instinctively by the wall, looking for a target. Jones turned his large electric torch toward the trunk. At the doorway he heard one of the outside men shout, "Harry," and saw the man's beam crisscross the barn and hunt high in the rafters and on the floor for some clue to the sudden darkness. For a moment there was silence except for the dog's barking, which had jumped an octave and sounded strangely like a human scream. The dog lunged out, snapping the leather leash his master held.

In the dark the bloodhound gave a yelp. The FBI man's light shifted just in time for Picard to see a great form in black gripping the big dog's hind legs and smashing its head to the floor with a nauseating bang.

The black form flitted across the floor toward the bales.

"Buster," screamed the Virginian, rushing to the dead dog.

"There he is, there he is," the man at the door shouted, and fired. Picard shot too, the reports banged hugely in the echo chamber of the barn. The flashlights darted toward the bales and two more spurts of fire from the FBI man's gun marked the gloom before the tall marauder disappeared among the bales.

Picard and the FBI man rose and plunged across the barn toward the hay, but before either had gone two steps, the dark figure stalked rapidly in front of them, directly past their light beams toward the trunk.

Jones shot first his beam, then his gun at the black-coated man. The man lifted a bale of hay over his head. His eyes blazed and his mouth opened in a scowl of hate as he brought it down toward the detectives. Picard, recognizing the attacker as Paulier despite his distorted features, got in a quick shot as the man exposed his chest, arms up in the air with the hay. But Paulier did not go down.

The hay struck Jones's shoulder as the FBI man flinched aside and the man in black swooped low to get at the trunk. Picard fired his last round, but the dark man had the trunk in the air in one hand as handily as another man might pick up an empty orange case.

It was then that Picard heard Pulanske's roar of anger from behind them, and saw the immense bulk of the homicide captain drive directly at the midsection of the man with the trunk.

Both men went down, but in a split second Picard in the light of his flashlight saw Pulanske's form hurled up from the tangle like a sack of potatoes. The beefy captain struck the floor with a grunt and writhed in agony.

Paulier scrambled from the floor, holding the trunk by the handle on one of its ends. Before Jones could fire, the man in black swung the chest at them. It whooshed past the heavy-set FBI man, who then hit the attacker at his thighs with his powerful shoulders and all the drive he could generate. Paulier fell to the ground like a tree and Jones, cursing viciously, was on him, his huge arm rising in the flashes of light like a slow-motion piston and coming down on the fallen man with heavy thumps.

Paulier grunted. One of the detectives now had Pulanske's big electric hand floodlight on them, and Picard darted in at the two struggling men. He was immediately lifted off the floor with a push from Paulier's feet.

Picard rolled over in time to see the FBI man cock his arm and hit the man in black a terrific blow in the face with his fist. The "bock" sounded strange in the barn. But in an instant Paulier wrenched free and kneed Jones in the chest, knocking him unconscious across the trunk. The black-clad man rolled him off to the barn floor as if he were a bag of waste paper.

Picard and two other detectives jumped Paulier as he bent and reached for the trunk again. They brought him down on one knee, but he was up like a cat, grabbed one of the detectives bodily, and hurled him kicking at the man with the floodlight. He went down, throwing the area of the fight into near darkness.

The smaller flashlights picked him out and showed a confused semicircle of men with drawn pistols jockeying to get in a shot at Paulier. Picard moved in one more time, but Paulier shoved him backward and grabbed the trunk.

This time he started for the gaping hole in the floor through which the bales had been thrown. Picard recognized in a flash that through this hole lay the first floor, the muddy cow stalls, and escape through the unhinged first-level doors.

His right arm aching as if broken, Picard nonetheless snatched the fallen homicide captain's pistol from his belt holster and darted in front of Paulier to block his flight. He fired at Paulier's chest and the man in black stumbled but did not fall. The shots were having little or no effect.

Frenzied now, the detective threw the pistol at Paulier. It struck him full in his face, but the man brushed Picard aside, jumped through the hole and into the hay below. The trunk caught in a broken rafter and Paulier, in the dark below, tugged to free it.

Picard, hardly thinking, jumped down feet first on the straining man. As he did, the trunk pulled free, and Paulier, in the moment before Picard could right himself in the hay, flung back the lid. The flashlights of the detectives around the hole above picked out Paulier as he hurriedly stuffed handfuls of the earth from the trunk into his overcoat pockets. Then as one of the detectives fired at him, he wheeled and clutched Picard's good wrist.

"You did this," Paulier hissed at him, the first words he had said in the wild turmoil. And Picard, looking into the red, seemingly pupilless eyes, the streaked white face, and the great red mouth, ringed with animal-white teeth, felt a fear he had never known paralyze him.

The stink of the madman—a huge amplification of that in the trunk—overwhelmed him. Paulier dragged him by the arm through the rotten hay and mud toward the outside.

Picard knew that Paulier only wanted to get him outside the range of the pistols and lights to kill him, and he wriggled feebly to free himself, but the man's iron grip held him.

Behind him the homicide detective could hear grunts as two detectives dropped through the hole to his aid. Paulier released his aching arm for a moment to tear at a heavy pipe that once must have been a stall divider. It came clear with a shriek of metal, just as Pulanske, like a groggy ox, plowed into the man in black. Picard momentarily marveled at his chief's comeback, then leaped on the struggling men, now on the muddy dirt floor of the stalls.

Flashlights caught the sweep of their arms and their tangled limbs, as both detectives clung to Paulier's arm bearing the lead pipe. With a straining swing of his arm, the killer threw both detectives away from him, then started toward them with the deadly pipe length.

Picard, out of breath, could not rise, but he struggled to drag the semiconscious Pulanske away from the advancing killer. Flashlights of the other detectives played on Paulier's incensed face, but Picard and Pulanske were too close for them to risk shots.

"No, no," Picard could hear the other detectives screaming as they fought to free themselves from the hay. Picard knew it would be too late. Horror filled his heart as he saw the man's hideous face.

But Paulier stopped, the features, which had been contorted with an unspeakable rage, sagged into lines of fear. The fire of hatred left the eyes, and Paulier began to make guttural snorts as he backed against a supporting beam, the pipe in his slack hand.

Picard thought the shots had had their effect, but he saw that the focus of the madman's shocked eyes was on Pulanske. Picard turned his head toward the slumped homicide captain, whose shirt was ripped to the waist.

The lights of the detectives' flashlights had touched a tiny cross of gold on Pulanske's mud-fouled undershirt. The cross, on its thin golden chain, flickered in the artificial light, seeming to throw off minute sparks as the uneven rays struck it.

"Uhh, uhh," the madman sighed, expelling his breath in rasps. The detectives' voices were stilled. The animal sound of the killer's grunts and the panting of the exhausted men were the only sounds in the fetid atmosphere of the barn.

Paulier still stared at the spot of gold on the slumped

detective's chest. Then, with a snarl of fear and amazement, Paulier recovered from his shock. His wild eyes and open red maw showed unrestrainable terror as the glitter of the little gold cross played lightly on his face and clothes. As if struck, he staggered backward, then, ducking low, he ran. He bumped a brick column and collided heavily into the creaking old wood of a cow stall. With a scream of panic he blundered with slipping steps through a sagging door and disappeared into the mist outside.

Three detectives rushed past Picard and Pulanske and on outside in pursuit of the man. Picard did not move. He had almost died at the hands of a maniac. Something unaccountable had saved him. He could only gasp in breath in great heaving lungfuls.

Outside he heard the detectives fire three shots at the murderer and several cries of "There, there he is." Then there was nothing until other members of the police group came to his aid and helped him and the staggering Pulanske out of the door and back toward the house.

The drizzle brought him around. At the house both he and Pulanske refused an ambulance. The burly homicide captain was bruised and in pain, but he had no broken bones. Picard's arm ached, but he would not leave. It was almost dawn before the pursuers, who had been augmented by uniformed men, came back to the house.

Robley had led them and he roused Picard, who was dozing fitfully on the sofa. The detective came to a sitting position before he was fully awake, and one look at the thin, discouraged face of Robley told him that Paulier had escaped.

"Harry," said the older detective, "I can't believe it. I can't believe it. I know we got at least a couple of slugs in him in the barn and he still had enough pizzazz to outrun us. Could he wear a bulletproof? Christ, how can a guy be so strong? He was still running hard when we lost him on the road. We got to find some other way of catching the son of a bitch if we ever run on him again, concentrate fire on his head, maybe."

Jones, who had gone with the pursuers, fixed Picard with a weary, inquiring gaze.

"Harry, did I see what I thought I saw down there when he ran out? Did he run from that cross, or am I just a superstitious half-Mick Catholic that doesn't know what end is up?"

Picard closed his eyes and leaned back on the sofa. He was so tired, so bewildered. And it was so hard to know what was true.

"I saw the cross too, Will. I thought he was looking at it. I don't know. I don't know what it was."

Dawn was coming grayly to the farm. Montgomery County had sent out an urn of coffee, and they sat waiting for the daylight in the muddy living room of the house, drinking the coffee and speculating on the killer's amazing powers.

Pulanske was joined by Captain Goldberg, of Robbery, just after dawn, and Kellam, of Missing Persons, arrived a few minutes later.

"The papers have it yet?" Pulanske asked Goldberg when he arrived in the cluttered living room.

"Yep, the *Post* missed it clean last night, but the *News* and *Star* will have something in their first editions. The chief gave 'em as little as he could, but they got Montgomery County they can work on."

"Umm," said the aching Pulanske gloomily, and set to planning the search for Paulier. Only a tiny number of the men outside the supersquad knew Paulier's identity, and he wanted it to stay that way. The reporters might pick up the name Peterson from Pantelein's partner, but they could be warned that this looked like an alias. At all costs the picture must stay out of the papers. Publication of it surely would send Paulier deeply into hiding or out of the city for good.

Copies must be shown to employees at airports, at the bus and train stations as soon as possible, and a general printed description could be issued. Sooner or later the name and photographs would be made public, but not yet.

Every home in a five-mile radius of the farmhouse must be contacted. There were dogs on the way, but little hope of help from them. The Virginian, heartbroken over Buster, said that no other hound at Occoquan could be counted on to do as well. And the rain made the trail even more elusive.

Culverts, sand-storage bins, barns, silos, anyplace where the fugitive might have hidden himself must be searched—car trunks, cellars. The hospitals had been warned by one of the FBI men through his duty agent at headquarters to be on the lookout for serious bullet wounds. So far only one such wound had turned up—the victim was an aging janitor whose wife found him with another woman.

A thorough search of the house was more productive.

Shirts that they found were bought at Saltz's and Goldheim's, fine downtown stores. The suits came from a Baltimore factory-retail store, Swartz's. The three stores could be checked for possible second addresses. The investigators found needles and thread, a second iron, and three pairs of shoes. One bore a London label inside. One of the striped regimental neckties had the name of a Singapore store on it, reminding Picard to hurry the check on what points Paulier had touched in before he came to Quebec. It was to these cities that he might be seeking to return even now.

On the bathroom sink and on the pillow and top part of the sheets there were traces of blood. A test might indicate whether it came from one of his victims and perhaps which one. Except for the unmade bed, the killer was a reasonably tidy housekeeper. There was no evidence in the house of any of the women except for two dissimilar buttons of a fancy design found in the stove, and what looked like a charred garter snap. Nothing to show that Pantelein had been there could be found.

There were plenty of prints. As best as ID could make it, they matched what they got off the pipe in the barn. And yes, there were other prints, in the bedroom mostly and the bathroom, but they'd have to check them against Sophie's and Norma's and Pantelein's and whatever else they needed to be checked against. Everyone was grumpy from lack of sleep and from failure, Picard thought as he waited for Pulanske, Goldberg, and Kellam to finish talking so they could go into town.

At headquarters Pulanske, a shoulder muscle pulled badly by his fight with the incredibly powerful Paulier, was sent home by the police surgeon on duty.

Picard showered and ate a heavy breakfast. Clean-shaven and full of food, he felt better able to face the day without sleeping. Back in the supersquad room one of the younger men handed him the first edition of the *News*. The headline was raw:

POTOMAC MURDER SUSPECT
ELUDES POLICE, FBI NET

The way the story was written made it all sound like a comedy of errors. Picard was angered. They had done their best against an adversary with unimaginable strength and cunning. But his anger faded when he thought how J. Edgar Hoover would react. Furious, thought Picard, the FBI portrayed as parties to a Keystone Cops episode.

Picard smiled. He hoped that the four agents would not get in trouble.

The story pegged the raid on the search for Pantelein, but said flatly that the killer was a suspect in the other three cases.

The *Star* came in shortly with much the same material. It had interviewed Mrs. Pantelein, the missing lawyer's partner, and neighbors at the farm. The farm itself was blocked off by Montgomery police, but there was an enterprising aerial photograph of it in the *Star's* second edition.

The "mysterious foreign national" was played up heavily, but aside from the general description, which did not mention Paulier's name, there were no damaging revelations in either afternoon paper.

By 1 p.m. the shirts had been traced. The stores believed that a bundle of shirts this size—twelve at Saltz's, six at Goldheim's—had been ordered by telephone. Yes, the clerk remembered that the man had phoned to make sure the size and quantity were available.

They were for late pickup, 7 p.m., the clerk believed. Yes, it would have been quite dark out. The girl downstairs vaguely remembered a tall man in black picking them up. A photograph? Well, it could've been him.

Swartz's quickly tied the description of the suits to a man who had called in with his detailed measurements. How'd he know what they had in fabrics? They'd told him that they had this and that, and he'd said two good dark flannels, a dark blue and a dark charcoal, and a dark tweed. The clerk remembered laughing, thinking he was an undertaker or something. He picked them up on one of their late nights, but the girl that was on the pickup desk had quit since.

"At night," Picard said to himself. "This guy just works at night. Nobody ever gets hurt or sees him in the day."

But then he thought, With a face like that I'd stay out of people's way in the day too.

Picard's arm began to swell badly that afternoon. He started to go to the police surgeon's office, but the telephone stopped him. It was Goldberg looking for Pulanske, but Harry would do fine.

"We've found Pantelein," said the robbery captain, and there was an excitement in his voice that Picard recognized as saying more than just that the body had been found.

"What else?" the homicide detective asked.

"Harry, the guy's throat is ripped up like an animal had been at it. But no blood around it. We think the guy's been bled dry."

Picard felt the familiar tremor of horror like a warning cello note, deep and somber. Had Paulier torn at the man's throat with those great white teeth that he had bared at Picard only a few hours ago, when the detective had thought he would surely die at the killer's hands?

The body had been found in about four feet of loose dirt beneath a shallow drainage ditch that ran past the wall of the shed. The water running through the ditch had obliterated the signs of fresh digging. But a county policeman noticed a small, rain-smoothed mound of dirt beside the ditch, and when he threw out a few shovelfuls of dirt from the ditch, he found it less packed than he had expected and with the help of others dug until he found the corpse.

The county coroner was on the way to the scene. Picard located Doc Kip through his wife, and a supersquadman rushed them out to the farm. Picard's arm hurt badly. The body was still there, beside the pit from which it had been removed, but the county coroner had supervised the thorough removal of the gluey mud from the face, arms, and shins.

The dead white face with its hideous wound below contrasted grotesquely with the muddy scramble of clothes that covered the miserably dead attorney. Kip, after a courteous gesture to the county coroner, examined the body.

Then he turned to Picard and shook his head.

"I guess it's what we've come to expect, Harry," he said somberly. "This man has been drained of blood and apparently starved prior to his death. You can see the folds of skin hanging from his frame. He was no athlete, though, to begin with."

Doc Kip's trained eye found an old hematoma—a bruise—on his right temple. Enough to have knocked him out, the old coroner said.

Perhaps, the detective thought, Paulier had knocked his victim unconscious when he kidnaped him from Washington. Or did Paulier lure him out to the farm and strike him there for some other reason, say when he tried to escape?

The dead lawyer still wore the cheap suit he had on the night of his son's birthday. But his tie was gone. When Doc Kip gently poured water on the shirt, he found bloodstains beneath the mud. How long dead? A few days at most, the two doctors agreed.

Picard returned to police headquarters too late to see the surgeon, but his arm was throbbing heavily and was swollen and sensitive from the elbow to his wrist. Robley saw it, said, "C'mon, Harry," and took him to Washington Hospital Center, where he was admitted overnight for a fractured forearm and a thorough checkup.

Picard's hospital room had the luxurious freshness of starched sheets, clean white walls, and speckless windows. He awoke and looked out sleepily at the familiar old city. The apartments and towers were backdropped by April's pale, intense blue morning sky. The hospital's lawns were close-cut and dew wet, and the landscaped trees were solidifying into bright green from chartreuse. For the first time in so many days he was resting.

His arm hurt, pounded so that it reflected in some small pulse beneath his ear. But he felt that he had the pain under control. He understood it. Outside his room he could smell hot chocolate, a smell that took him back to his boyhood, a simpler if not a better time. He shuffled from his room.

The nurse promised him a cup of chocolate and newspapers. Dutifully he returned to his bed and crawled in. When the *Post* came he unfolded it eagerly, then gasped at its front page.

A two-column picture of Paulier stared out at him. But it was with the dead eyes of the passport photograph, not the wild eyes that had threatened him two nights ago. The eight-column headline told him of Pantelein's body being found. But it was the "deck" headline that held him:

COUNTY CORONER CITES 'VAMPIRISM'

Picard read the article. Apparently last night the chief had yielded to the pressure of the newspapers and released a good deal of material on the first two deaths as well as most of the Pantelein data. Paulier's name was given, but he was identified only as "a British citizen."

Well, thought Picard bitterly, it probably couldn't be helped. The guy will fly away now to plague somebody else. But he'll get caught. Whatever ails him, he can't stop it, he has to keep killing.

He looked back at the paper. They really have a sensation on their hands now, don't they? he thought. Wade Brazille, the medical reporter for the *Post,* had a front-page article at the bottom of the page on "vampirism." There was also a feature story on the vampire legend, based on an apparently hurried reading of *Dracula* and remembrances of late-late shows on television.

Brazille's article interested Picard. It was speculative

but conservative and was based on talks with medical authorities.

"Whether Franklin Pantelein was bled to death, or whether as sensation-lovers have speculated his killer actually drank some of his blood, the bizarre disease apparently behind his death is not unknown to medical science," the article began.

"Hemothymia, pseudovampirism, or vampirism are the names variously given it, but its basic symptom is the same: the person afflicted has an uncontrollable desire to see or taste the blood of another, generally for reasons associated with sex.

"In its most extreme form, the patient actually believes himself to be a vampire, that is, a body that is risen from the grave and that feeds by sucking the blood of the living.

"Some doctors feel the current rash of vampire movies shown on television and in theaters may have made critical a condition that lies dormant in a surprising number of people."

Picard wondered how the television stations would feel about that. He read on:

"Dr. Montague Summers, the late author of *The Vampire, His Kith and Kin* (University Books, Inc.), reported a case in 1894 in which a father, thirty, bit his daughter on her lips and hands and sucked her blood 'because he loved it.'

"More recently, a young clerk in London was convicted of murder and hanged after confessing that he killed several persons in his basement, tapped their bodies for a glass of blood, then disposed of them in drums of sulphuric acid.

"The disease is generally found, psychiatrists here say, in paranoid persons—those who have acute delusions that they are being persecuted.

"One prominent psychiatrist, who asked that his name be withheld, said:

" 'Without assessing the present case, I would say that anyone suffering from a so-called vampire delusion would probably be classed as extremely psychotic—unable to control his compulsion for blood.' "

And so on, Picard thought glumly. If we did catch him he would be not guilty by reason of insanity and I'd be paying taxes to keep him in the nut house for the rest of his life and mine.

He put down the paper and turned on the television set, seeking later news of the case. A kiddy show was on. He watched listlessly as an adult in a funny hat talked inanely of a plastic tommy-gun set. Then the show suddenly blipped out, and a local news cut-in came on.

A ten-state lookout was being broadcast for Paulier on a warrant charging him with the murder of Pantelein. He was also wanted for assault with intent to kill on the several police officers and as an accessory in the murders of Sophie Matlack and Norma Heldwig.

The announcer gave his description as a "European national, possibly posing as a businessman or produce man," and then Paulier's ugly face popped upon the screen.

Blown up until it was almost useless on the screen, the old passport photo looked out at Picard with a strange, bright passiveness.

Nonetheless the thin nose and the dead, slightly closed eyes of the photo set his heart to beating fast. The announcer droned on ... "no clues ... a search failed to reveal ... investigations continue ...," the old clichés. Picard turned off the television set. He wished that he had another cup of hot chocolate. But when he got it, there was none of the contentment that the first cup had brought him.

The doctors told him that he had a greenstick fracture, and set his arm. They X-rayed him, pronounced him sound, and ordered him to stay in bed until afternoon and away from work for a day or two. Picard, discouraged, obliged. That evening he checked out of the hospital and caught a cab across the city to his home.

In the morning he called Susy. She had not walked Friday night because of the rain. She had walked Saturday night just in case, but it had seemed futile, with Paulier's picture all over the place. No, she did not know what they wanted her to do next.

Yes, she would like to go out with him tonight, but she couldn't because she was taking the boy to visit with his father's mother in Richmond. Yes, she said, laughing at his flippant question, she would miss him somewhat.

Picard got up and dressed, pulling a sport shirt and sweater gingerly over his light cast. He walked the two miles from his apartment to the Library of Congress.

He looked up "Vampire" in the file, and there, card after card, in English and French, German and Swedish, Rumanian and Latin, were books on the subject.

He picked the book by Dr. Summers mentioned in the *Post*; a translation of a court proceeding; an 1860 translation by some preacher of Calmet, Augustin; *Vampires and Vampirism,* by Wright, Dudley; and a half-dozen other volumes.

Flicking on the light at his desk in the high-ceilinged old room, he felt as if he were again a student those many years ago at the University of Maryland.

The court proceeding, his first venture, was translated in a thick book on criminal psychoses and dealt with a man named Fritz Haarmann of Hanover, Germany. Haarmann had been hospitalized as a youth for some mental disease. After World War I, he opened a butcher shop in Hanover, sold stolen meat, and protected himself from arrest by informing on perverts to the police.

At that time, Picard read, Hanover was a center for homosexuals, and Haarmann frequented the third-class waiting rooms at railway stations in search of runaways to whom he offered a place to sleep. Thereafter many of the youths disappeared, but they went unnoticed in those troubled times. Finally, a perverted debauch led to his arrest and police extracted from him a confession that he had killed at least twenty-seven youths.

The forty-six-year-old butcher recited how he held down his victims by biting deeply into their throats. Some of the youths he ate, Picard read to his astonishment; others he butchered, selling parts of them in his shop. The bones and some bodies he threw into the canal. Police testified that they dredged and found skulls and femurs as well as some entire skeletons.

Haarmann was executed on April 15, 1925, by having his head cut off with a sword, an ancient punishment reserved for the most hideous crimes.

Picard noted the medical comments: "A rare case of pseudovampirism . . . suggest diagnosis that subject wished to be caught so he could be punished [not for crimes, but] for some early homosexual activity suppressed because of parental strictness . . . stalked his victims only nocturnally . . . as disease progressed, note subject spent increasing daylight hours in bed behind his closed shop . . . described his sleep as 'my trance' . . ."

Picard picked up another volume and leafed through it. Paulier's face: how well it fitted the description of a vampire, lips "blub and red," thin, rapacious nose, large white predatory teeth, fiery-eyed when angered, dead-eyed when surfeited.

God, he thought, if I'd been born as ugly as Paulier, maybe I'd think I was some kind of vampire too.

He read on. The vampire lies in the grave forty days after his burial, then leaves it to batten on the living. Those who are bitten by the vampire first come under his control, then languish and wither as he feeds on their blood until they die. Their appetites fade, then utterly disappear as they themselves become the vampire's fare.

Picard felt sick. Had Paulier hypnotized his victims and then gradually drunk their lifeblood as they lay in bed at the farm under his complete control? Had they lost all desire for food as part of this hideous ritual?

He thought of Sophie's lost look as she passed the professor . . . the dreamlike gaze of Norma Heldwig as the bellhop escorted her to her fatal ride . . . the dreadful loss of blood, of weight as if from starvation . . .

Picard started. Here, in an old translation, a Hungarian reported the vampire's strength "liken to that of eight stout wights." Picard's arm ached within the cast at the memory of Paulier's steel-trap grip.

The mythical being had the power in one legend to turn into a mist. In another all those who died of his attacks themselves became vampires . . . Picard found ways of dispatching the "undead"—cut off his head with a sexton's shovel, with a sword (good God, Haarmann, he thought), steal his shroud, lay a wild rose on his coffin, burn him, stuff his mouth with rocks and garlic, ring his casket with a paste of holy wafers, expose him to light, shoot him with a blessed silver bullet, drive an ash or hawthorn stake through his heart.

Picard wondered whether he would ever get another shot at the killer with his own steel-jacketed bullets. He would shoot for the head, as Robley suggested, where no bulletproof vest could protect the killer.

It was in the thin book by Wright that he read with an uneasy sense of recognition of the cross as a specific against vampires. He looked up from the book, seeing again the twisted terror on the face of the man who had been ready to kill him with a pipe. Could it truly be that Pulanske's little golden cross had so terrified him?

Other books told him of fantastic old wives' weapons

for fending off vampires. There were garlic, Bibles, the sign of the cross, pictures of the Madonna or of Jesus. Another quaint entry told of the genesis of the Slavic vampire:

". . . through the coming together of the Devil, which was in his primeval form, the serpent, that is the viper or adder, and a vile Witch, she also like the serpent in her evil."

The vampire generally hated sunlight, Picard read. He detested mirrors, for he could not see his image in them. The vampire myth, he read further, originated in Eastern Europe in the seventeenth century, and superstition spread it throughout the Continent, where it dwindled in the mid-eighteenth century. Periodically there were new flurries of the old belief in isolated mountain areas down to this day. But these were short-lived and as uncommon as some plague that lies dormant for decades, even centuries, only to crop out suddenly and vanish as quickly.

Picard jotted down notes on his reading as if he were taking a police report from a witness whose story he doubted.

The books told him that the "undead" slept in their coffins or other dark places during the day and had to have beneath them the soil of their native churchyard. The thought snapped Picard up from the book. The earth, this was why the psychotic Paulier had stuffed the earth in his pocket, indeed had perhaps carried it all the way from wherever he originated.

In Montague Summers' classic work he found a mention of the vampire's reek. The odor of the charnel house, that was the way the British occultist described it. Picard sniffed again the decay smell of the trunk, recalled Roticella's description.

Charnel Number Five, he thought gruesomely.

That Paulier dealt with the dead was unmistakable. Did he feed on other corpses as well? It was too horrible to contemplate.

The vampire, he read, left only two small holes in the throat of his victim, the places where his extended hollow canine teeth pierced. Paulier had cut or rended the throats of the three persons Picard knew he had killed.

Only in this detail, Picard thought, has he failed to play the role with precision. And a small voice inside him thought, Thank God there is one thing at least that makes him human, however awful it is.

The detective's eyes burned from the hours of unaccustomed reading. He thought of all the books in the library on vampires, in French, in German, in all the languages he would never know. He wished uneasily that he had gotten a full education, then, picking up his pad with its schoolboy-handwriting notes, he left the old library.

Down the hill he walked in the sunshine. The perfect white dome of the Capitol was behind him, substantial, intelligent, and reassuring. Here was the familiar peculiarly moist air that envelops Washington on some spring days. Here were the sidewalks, the shapely street lamps on the Capitol Hill walkways, the annual bursting of green foliage on tree and bush, the things he knew, expected, understood. Vampire stories in the twentieth century, how silly. And yet the quarry, Paulier, was real and rooted through his warped mind to the centuries-old myths, the dark lore of the malign and arcane vampire.

That night Picard stayed in his room, tired and weak from the long days of activity. He lay in bed and read the book he had picked up in the library's special book-loan section. It was *Dracula,* but he found the old-timey writing too much for his sleepy mind. As he dropped off he wondered if there would be a run on garlic and crosses. So much, too much, publicity on this vampire business. God, that bastard had been strong, he thought as his arm gave one last throb.

★

The next morning a State Department security officer called to tell Picard that the British report on Paulier from Malaya had arrived and been delivered—through channels—to State.

The report was so damned screwy that maybe Picard would like to wait for the one from our own people anyway before he took any action on it, said the State Department man. How screwy? He would see when he read it. He was sending over copies of the material with a courier right now.

While Picard waited, he glanced at the material the supersquad had developed during the last few days when he had been concentrating on the raid—and on his recovery from the assault.

Quebec customs had found that Paulier came in from London on a night flight. Nothing in the least out of the way as far as they could determine.

The Canadians had located three passengers and the crew. It had been a quiet but crowded flight and no one had seen anyone like the picture.

The hundred fifty pounds overweight showed up on the flight from London; yes, cash paid for all the tickets.

At London the trail ended. Paulier had bought the ticket to Quebec the night the plane left. That was all London knew at present, but they were still checking.

Pulanske came in and moments later the State Department courier arrived with the British material. The homicide captain walked into his office with a manila envelope, tearing it open as he went. Picard sat by him, reading along, as Pulanske concentrated on the report with his head cupped in his left hand.

The report was in three parts, two from the Malayans and one assessing the material from the British diplomatic officer who had dealt with the Malayans in developing the data on Paulier.

The first Malayan report, based solely on official documents, contained only a few mystifying bare facts.

Paulier, it recorded, had arrived in George Town, on the Malayan west coast, sometime in 1950. Exactly when was unknown because the hectic times surrounding independence had occasioned gaps in the records. He filed papers as a resident alien in a little inland rubber community near the coastal town of Bandar Maharani, in late 1950. In these he listed himself as manager of a rubber plantation that he leased from its absentee owner, a German who lived in George Town.

Tax records showed that he paid his levies promptly and was apparently making a fairly good profit on the plantation. His visa was regularly renewed in Kuala Lumpur, the capital.

One cryptic entry showed up: "Socialist party requests investigations conditions Johorenberg plantation and activities lessee-manager S. Paulier, Oct. 2, 1962."

The final date in the first section of the Malayan file was Nov. 1, 1962, when he flew to Singapore.

The second report, also from Malayan authorities, was headed "Confidential" and a handwritten cover sheet stated that permission for any release of the information should be requested through the nearest Malayan diplomatic office. The report read:

"The following information on British citizen Sebastian Paulier, former resident of Johorenberg, near Bandar Maharani, Johore, is provided solely for the use of the British High Commissioner.

"S. Paulier, contrary to rumor in Johore, was the subject of only a single official complaint. It came from Membran S. B. Sanduan, secretary of the Socialist party, Malacca. Mr. Sanduan said that although pay at Johorenberg was adequate—even higher than on surrounding plantations— other conditions had become seriously below acceptable standards.

"As of Oct. 2, 1962 (the day of Mr. Sanduan's report), he reported that the following conditions prevailed:

"1. Corporal punishment was practiced by order of the lessee and at the hands of a 'gestapo-like' force of extremely well paid single males. These persons policed other workers and served as a bodyguard for S. Paulier.

"2. Health standards were low and medical facilities not provided by the lessee. As a consequence the infant mortality rate was well above the national average.

"3. The vicious actions of the bodyguards and of S. Paulier on several occasions inspired near-panic in the workers. Absence of other employment in the area, alone, kept workers at Johorenberg.

"Mr. Sanduan asked for an investigation by the Health Ministry and by the constabulary. This was considered at Kuala Lumpur, but it was decided that a summary of Mr. Sanduan's allegations would first be sent to the absentee owner and to S. Paulier.

"This was done. The absentee owner, Herr Claus Witschenbach, who holds other properties in the republic, notified the Foreign Ministry and Health Ministry on Oct. 25 that S. Paulier was no longer the manager-lessee and that he understood S. Paulier was leaving the federation. Herr Witschenbach, furthermore, informed the ministries that he was sending a new manager to the plantation within a week. This closed the matter as far as the republic was concerned."

Picard and Pulanske leafed on to the next two pages of the material. It was in the form of a confidential memorandum to the State Department from the British Embassy in Washington, and was titled "Report, H.M. Foreign Ministry, London, from K. Stokes Johnsyme, Kuala Lumpur."

The curious document was a strange mixture of unconfirmed reports, detailed investigation, and Malay scholarship. This picture emerged:

Johnsyme, a security employee of the consulate in Kuala Lumpur, made a routine request to the Malayan Foreign Ministry on being asked to investigate the case by London.

The first brief and enigmatic report from Malayan authorities was the result.

Johnsyme pressed harder, stressing that the man was a suspect in a murder and that time was of the essence. The Malayan Foreign Ministry then produced the second report, fuller, but still not satisfying the curious Englishman on all points.

Johnsyme, however, had an associate, the most vocal Labour supporter on the consular staff, who called Sanduan. A meeting was arranged in Malacca. There Sanduan, a dedicated labor organizer, told Johnsyme frankly that something other than bad treatment had occurred up there in Johorenberg.

It was true, Sanduan acknowledged, that some of the stranger complaints against Paulier had come from among the most superstitious of the plantation workers.

But Sanduan's talks with more reliable workers proved to him that infant mortality was very high, higher than even unsanitary and poor nutritional conditions could explain. Fear was everywhere among them.

Over the years Paulier had become an increasingly willful taskmaster. Not infrequently he would show up from nowhere at night and break into the circle of a fire to drag off some hapless Malayan whose minor infraction during the day had been reported to him. The man, sometimes hours later, would stagger back to the fire, or into his hut, weeping and bleeding from lashes and awed by the ferocity and strength of Paulier.

Paulier, himself, said Sanduan, apparently worked only at night, often all night long, as the light in his room attested. During the day he slept in a room that was locked even from his own bodyguards.

Among themselves, the workers called him *pennang-galan*, *pelesit*, or sometimes *bajang*, old superstitious terms for demons. Not one regretted his departure.

Since the arrival of a new manager, Sanduan continued, the conditions had improved, particularly for the infants. There was every sign that the vast plantation was recovering from Paulier's tenure.

Johnsyme pressed Sanduan on the *pennanggalan*, the *pelesit*, and *bajang*—this last a word he had heard applied by country Malayans to Westerners generally. But Sanduan uncomfortably laughed off his questions, and Johnsyme flew back that evening with his Labour party friend.

The friend, Harvey by name, had served in Malaya and the old Straits Settlements for years, from way before the war, and had an amateur's interest in its folklore.

"The *pennanggalan* and *pelesit* are all but gone," he told Johnsyme on the flight back. "They're part of ancient back country superstitions, and when the terms are used now, they're just to describe a thoroughly bad man."

The *pennanggalan*, a head with entrails attached, was originally a malevolent being, male or female, who after a particularly evil life turns to glutting itself on the blood of the newly born. The cries of a newly born babe drive it wild with blood lust. As it sweeps shimmeringly through the forest it drips blood, and anyone who is touched by the fluid is blighted with skin afflictions.

The *pennanggalan*'s screech, an unearthly, penetrating note, is the warning to all households where a birth is imminent to hang up thistles or thorns inside and out. The *pennanggalan* is in terror of catching its intestines in the thorns. In the nineteenth century the carefully nourished rose gardens of English diplomats' wives frequently were destroyed by natives seeking thistles to ward off demons. The wild-rose sprigs of European vampire lore! Picard recalled as he read.

How had the myth arisen? Well, Harvey did not know, but he suspected that it sprang from the *ignis fatuus*—the will-o'-the-wisp fires—in the marshes of southern Malaya. The weird dance of the burning gases would account for the shimmering intestines. Then, it was true that in the old days the infant mortality of the straits had been incredibly high, even by Asian standards.

And that was the end of Johnsyme's report.

The final enclosure in the British packet was a brief note that Scotland Yard had checked Paulier's old addresses in London, at least those where the buildings had not been torn down. The most interesting fact was how little anyone at the houses knew of the man. A sort of "night person," one landlady recalled. He had not rented from landlords who lived on the premises. The man who vouched for him on his naturalization papers could not be located, but the Yard had some reason to believe he made a business of "professional vouching" for refugees and others some ten years ago.

The Yard had sought in vain for Paulier's route from Malaya, which the first Malay report said he left November 1. They did not know what he had done between then and December 15, when he flew from London to Quebec.

Pulanske finished the reports and looked up at Picard.

"That clinches it, Harry," said Pulanske. "If we were ever worried about our man using the British or Malayan or whatever guy's identity, we can stop worrying now. Christ, we really got some kind of nut on our hands," he added, tapping a knuckle on the desk. "You talked to any psychiatrists about this pseudovampirism complex?"

No, said Picard. Better had, said Pulanske.

Picard told the homicide captain about his visit to the library. Pulanske listened carefully to the old tales, capsuled by Picard, nodding as they applied to Paulier.

"The books tell you everything about them except

how to catch them," Picard said. "You know, it may sound screwy, but I think if I could find out how to catch a story-book vampire, I could catch this guy.

"When I was reading this stuff, I had the damnedest feeling that this guy had read it all too, and maybe all the books in Latin and German and Christ knows what else—that he's read so much he knows just how a vampire behaves. And he's a genius enough to live like a vampire does and still give us the slip."

Picard recalled that one of the medical studies, the one that dealt with the Hanoverian butcher, he thought, had used the phrase "psychologically wedded to his role."

The homicide detective looked at Pulanske to see how he was reacting to this unorthodox theory. The big captain pressed his lips together and nodded his head heavily.

"I believe you, Harry. I believe you," he grunted. "I never thought I'd see a case like this, but I never thought I'd see a lot of screwy cases."

"Why'd he put the trunk in the hay, do you think?" asked Pulanske.

"Dunno. Maybe he kept it there when he wasn't traveling. You know, he could've been in a town all night, then holed up in a hotel all day, sleeping inside that trunk. He's got that damned dirt in there, like in the old stories. Lord knows where it came from, the dirt. For all I know he crawled in the trunk every night. He could have moved enough bales on the side in an hour to edge in there, maybe. You saw how strong he is."

Pulanske interrupted. "Or maybe he gives up the vampire bit when it's inconvenient for him and sleeps in a bed all day just like any other night person, sunlight or no sunlight. Maybe he just plays the game when he thinks he can get away with it. . . . All I know is that he sure as hell came back and took a chance to get that dirt, so he must be crazy enough to really believe he had to have it. . . ."

"It didn't say in the books what happened if they didn't sleep on the dirt," Picard observed gloomily. "Smashing the mirrors is funny too," he continued. "Vampires can't see themselves in a mirror, so they get rid of mirrors. With this guy, when he looks in a mirror he sees himself and it makes him feel like he's not a real vampire. Maybe that's why he hates mirrors."

The afternoon papers arrived. The vampire story was on the front page again. The *Star* had discovered Roticella, who had been unable to resist the publicity.

The drama of the night purchase had taken on even more sinister colors in Roticella's mind since the story broke:

"He glided toward me without a sound . . . the whole room felt like he chilled it, iced it with his very presence . . ." These were two of the used-car dealer's more elaborate quotes.

There was little else talked about in the city. Every new stabbing brought fears that it had been done by the "vampire." The women particularly were frightened.

With all three female victims blondes, this shade of hair, once so prevalent among the young dye-prone government girls, had become almost extinct.

Excitement was heightened when the *Star* feature writer Mockley duplicated Picard's reading at the Library of Congress and used it for a much-discussed article. He dealt with the specifics against vampires—garlic, crosses, rose sprigs, holy medals. It was written tongue-in-cheek with touches of humor. Picard was surprised that the paper printed an article with this light approach when at least three persons had been killed. But there was perhaps one virtue: if one did put garlic around his neck, would not Paulier leave that person alone? Very likely.

Would the superstitious tear up their neighbors' rose gardens, as in Malaya? How similar were the Asian *pen-*

nanggalan and the European vampire, how surprisingly similar, he mused.

Mockley followed up his own story the next day with the reaction to it. Sales of garlic in the city went up. The religious objects shops reported a run on crucifixes. A priest said that a woman had raided his holy water font with a Mason jar. Another told of the theft of a carton of holy wafers, apparently by a parishioner anxious for a potent charm against the vampire.

Picard himself, one afternoon, quietly bought a small gold crucifix and a cheap gold-plated chain. After he had paid for it, he returned to the showcase and bought another—for Susy.

Meanwhile the dogged, dreary work went on of checking leads, corresponding with other police forces, and waiting for some new break.

On Capitol Hill several senators and a dozen or so congressmen had discreetly called their colleagues on the District committees of the Senate and the House. These, in turn, contacted the police chief, and by the end of the day officers found their assignments changed to patrolling homes of the worried members of Congress.

But there was no legislative cure for the fear that hung in the clear spring air, that emptied downtown streets and brought locks to doors that had for decades been left trustingly open of nights.

Time magazine did a story on the slayings (it was thought too alarming for the cover). "Lights burned late at the Mussolini-modern headquarters of Washington's police force . . ." it began.

A liberal magazine had the temerity to blame J. Edgar Hoover for failure to solve the crimes, and four Republicans and three Democrats immediately defended the FBI head in the *Congressional Record*.

All vampire movies were taken off all three major television networks, to much fanfare by the networks about their sense of public service. A science fiction film called *The Blood of Saturn* had its name changed to *Planet Zero*.

Reporters tied up the lines to the homicide squad until Pulanske had the switchboard weed them out and refer them to the chief's office, where sketchy announcements were sent to keep the press satisfied. The foreign news corps, particularly the French, insisted on interviews with Pulanske, but with no good news to report Pulanske's earlier love for publicity quickly soured.

No new clue, no reappearance, no new victim of Paulier had turned up in Washington, in Baltimore, or indeed anywhere. Gradually the publicity began to die down.

Susy had suspended her streetwalking for two weeks.

Pulanske, more out of fear of criticism than a belief that her vigil would have results, asked her to go back to the Crowley-Shelton on the evening of a big restaurateurs' convention. She agreed reluctantly. The futility of her march had annoyed her, and she resolved to find a way to avoid future assignments to the role.

Picard met her downtown that night for dinner. She had not made up her face except for light lipstick. When she came into Blackie's, where Picard waited for her, he marked her shortened dress and prostitute's spike heels. This masquerade contrasted with the good unpainted planes of her face in a way that made her more attractive than ever for him.

He got up as she approached the table.

"You show pretty nice manners to us girls of the night," she said, and made a suggestion of a curtsy. Then she took his hand for a moment as she sat. But he sensed she was nervous.

"You look beautiful, Susy," he said with awkward seriousness.

"Oh Harry, please," she said with a slight edge in her voice, then, sensing that he was hurt, she continued, "Let's not talk about that, about each other. It's so complicated, this working on the case together, and thinking about . . . liking each other at the same time."

She stopped, but felt she had not reassured him in the way she had meant to do.

"I'm going to be here tomorrow and the next day, Harry. I'm not going anywhere," she finished more graciously.

Picard was a patient detective and a patient man. He knew that she had weighed him, found him what he was, and accepted him: hard-working, not overly imaginative, as tough as he ought to be. One who would be honest with her.

"Do you think this man will show up again?" she asked.

"I don't know," he replied. "Maybe he did, somewhere out of town. Or maybe he stayed here; there could be somebody in the river right now, or the bay or the Baltimore Harbor. The case is full of maybes."

Susy absorbed what he said, but continued quietly.

"Maybe he'll think things have blown over a bit. Maybe he will venture out. And I'm the only blonde left in town for him. . . . Oh Harry," she said, giving her head a shake, "I'll be so glad when it's all over."

"You've picked up a new profession, anyway," he said to brighten her, but the joke was becoming a tired one.

She said nothing, then sighed, "We'd better start."

Picard, Robley, and two Third Precinct men assigned to help watch Susy dropped her off at the Crowley-Shelton and pulled up into the hotel driveway.

The four men were armed with forty-five-caliber automatics against the vaunted strength of the killer, rather than with their ordinary service revolvers and detective specials. One of the huge uniformed men—now clad in oversized civilian clothes—bore a longshoreman's hook.

He had heard of Paulier's impermeable vest. The other carried a short-range tear-gas dispenser, and all carried short ugly lengths of pipe instead of blackjacks.

Picard fingered the little cross within his shirt. He had meant to ask Susy if she was wearing the one he had given her. It seemed an age since they had begun this surveillance. The days and the nights of the investigation had run together and he was tired all the time.

Robley was nervous too. They watched the crowds on Sixteenth Street strolling past the marquee of the big hotel. The women's legs, made trim and firm by their heels and stockings, shone as they flicked past the lights of the Crowley-Shelton. The airline limousine pulled up, discharged its travelers, and left. The evening was heavy, dark—May rain clouds waited warmly between earth and the moon.

Susy's mastery of the slightly slouched promenade of the whore set Picard to musing. Did she practice it consciously, or did a woman simply fall into it naturally when she walked too long in heels on concrete? Whatever the case, the walk threw her buttocks against the thin summer coat she wore: step, curve, step, curve, step, curve. Who could resist something like that? he thought with a slight smile to himself.

Susy was two hundred feet away when she made her turn and started back toward Picard's unmarked cruiser. In a shadowed area between a street light and the flaring marquee a man moved out from near a hedge. Picard jarred Robley with his elbow and Robley put his hand on the door handle, ready to spring it.

The man, clad in black, with a slouch hat, walked with light, jerky steps. It was Paulier.

The four men, hoping to be on him before he spotted them, sprang noiselessly from the car and separated as they walked rapidly toward the sidewalk.

In the slightly shadowed area, Paulier met Susy. She turned to him with a quick, frightened look. Picard could see the scene clearly as he approached the couple.

The man in black appeared to look directly into Susy's frozen face from about two feet away. Instead of turning from him, she swayed almost against him for an instant as if drawn by a magnet, then stumbled back and swayed toward him again.

Paulier, still staring, took her arm quickly. She offered no resistance. Even at a distance Picard could see her face wrinkle with concentration. For a split second more, Paulier stared into her eyes. She seemed caught by his gaze. Suddenly, with an expression of disgust and surprise, Paulier switched his glance to the approaching detectives as if Susy had given him some silent warning. His look of surprise flashed into anger, and Picard saw the roll of those red eyes that had terrified him in the barn.

With quick, stilted steps the man in black broke for the hotel. Susy gave Picard a wild look, then staggered and turned to sit on the low wall that ran along the sidewalk.

Picard paused a moment. His instinct told him that she could not be hurt badly and that the man must be caught now or he would again escape. Robley was ahead of him as they dashed across the narrow lawn in an attempt to head off Paulier before he reached the hotel doorway.

With a single snarl of white teeth the man hurried into the hotel. The two detectives banged through the door just in time to see the man in black—followed by the stares of ten or twenty persons—striding through the lobby. He turned left toward the corridor to the men's bar.

Picard had passed Robley. His forty-five in hand, he ran like a halfback through the lobby chairs and the hotel guests, who fell back from the pursuers. All he could think of was reaching the madman again.

Behind him a man shouted, "Stop him! Stop him!"

above the screams of women affrighted by the guns and the Third Precinct man's drawn cargo hook. Paulier sped past the men's bar.

Picard rounded a corridor corner behind the fleeing Paulier and saw with a thrill that the entire end of the corridor was blocked with men, heavy-set delegates to the restaurateurs' convention. But with a quick flash of his black chesterfield Paulier darted into a door near the men's room sign.

"Take the first door," Picard shouted back to the other detectives. Robley quickly tried it, then the gigantic Third Precinct man smashed into it with his shoulder. The man was drawing back for a second drive at it as Picard swung open the next door down the hall—the men's room.

Picard, out of breath, rushed into the room close to the doorjamb. He steadied his pistol arm against his side as he burst around a partition and into the tiled room. Goddamit, he cursed, no one. He kicked the door of the first stall open, then that of the second. He kicked the third, but it refused to give.

"What the hell . . ." a voice in the stall began. Picard crouched and looked beneath the door, where a pair of gray trousers were fast being pulled up. It was not their man.

The room was windowless. In the upper part of the wall was a grilled ventilator. Picard leaped to the top of a urinal and jerked at the ventilator, but it was firm, the paint uncracked where it met the wall. The grillwork was damp with condensation.

Picard stood panting for a moment. The bastard was gone unless they'd found him next door. He ran back into the hall and pushed rudely through the stunned faces of guests blocking the two doorways.

The room next door was a storage room; its door now hung on one hinge. Inside, the two precinct men were trying to jimmy the closet open with the cargo hook. The padlocked door was metal-reinforced.

"Get the key, for Christ sake," he ordered one of them as he brushed past them to the single window. Robley was working at it with his bare hands. Between the two of them they removed the heavy wood-framed screening that covered it on the inside. The casement window was closed but not locked. Certainly it was big enough for a man's escape. Could Paulier have jerked loose the screening, opened the window, and then ground it shut in so short a time? That was the only possibility.

The assistant manager bustled in with the key to the closet padlock, and Picard worked at the lock while Robley stood back from the door with his automatic cocked. Even with the padlock on the outside he was taking no chances. The lock clicked open and Picard heaved the door open wide. Robley tensed, then relaxed. Nothing but cartons and canned goods.

Robley ran to post a lookout, while Picard combed the room for any evidence that Paulier had passed through. He murmured to one of the officers to call Identification at once for a check of the window for prints.

Outside the room the guests packed the hall. A hotel aide was pushing them back while two bellboys vainly tried to set up an ornate gold-threaded rope on two small stanchions. The talk was a roar. Word had traveled up and down the dignified hotel's corridors that the "vampire killer" had been spotted in the hotel.

Picard picked out one of the heavy-set men who had been at the end of the hall. He gripped his arm.

"You saw him go in one of these rooms?" he demanded.

"Yeah, the bathroom, I think the bathroom," the man stammered. "He got out? Say, who was that guy?"

Picard did not answer, but turned again to the men's room.

The place smelled strongly of disinfectant, but above this pervasive odor was there another, subtler one, the distinctive long-dead smell of Paulier? He could not tell. He wiped his sweating forehead, and as his palm passed his nose, there it was, the smell, on his hand. Had he picked it up on the ventilator? On the window frame in the storage room? He sniffed both spots, but if the odor had once clung momentarily to either, it was now dissipated forever.

Outside a scout car was pulled up on Sixteenth Street and a Third Precinct man was questioning two sailors. Picard looked anxiously for Susy.

"Where is she?" he asked brusquely of the uniformed men. They looked up disagreeably, then became attentive when they recognized the homicide sergeant.

"These boys say an ambulance took her," said one of the men, nodding at the sailors. "They don't know what happened. She was just sitting on the wall with her head in her hands. We heard the lookout and the policeman-in-trouble call on the way over. What happened, Sergeant?"

Picard answered shortly, "Assault on a policewoman," then told him to get all the witnesses he could find. A Second Precinct detective cruiser roared up with its siren screaming.

"Where'd he go, Harry?" shouted the white-haired detective lieutenant from the Second.

"I don't know, Brad," said Picard. "Can you get some people in the hotel looking around? Robbie's in there. There's some fat guys that saw the bastard. You can't miss them."

The white-haired man sprang sprily from the car and walked long-legged toward the hotel, while his partner called headquarters to send more searchers. Other police cars arrived, the inevitable result of a policeman-in-trouble call. We take care of our own, Picard thought, greeting the grim, familiar faces.

Picard called Communications from his own cruiser and found that Susy had been taken to the Hospital Center. He notified the dispatcher that he was going there. Perhaps he should have stayed and briefed Pulanske, but he was worried about Susy. He could justify his absence by the need of a full report from her.

The blond policewoman was sitting in the low-ceilinged anteroom of the emergency section. In the fluorescent light, her face looked pale and frightened beneath the heavy coating of make-up. Picard saw her there, forlorn, disquieted before she looked up and smiled with recognition. The curve of her lips gave way to an expression curiously mixing trust and need. He felt a sharp hurt mingled with . . . with what? love for her, he supposed.

The detective sat down on the bench beside her, not taking her hand, as he wanted to, because of the nurses and the two other policemen there on their own cases.

"What happened, baby?" he asked softly.

"Oh, it was too awful, Harry. I'm so scared," she moaned, then she brightened somewhat, diverted by the sound of her own childish remorse.

"When I got here," she continued in a tense and sad little voice that still laughed a bit at itself, "I was waiting for an examination and some woman whose husband had hit her was sitting next to me. So when I put my head down—I guess I felt faint—she said, 'What's the matter, honey, you pregnant or something?' "

"It seemed so funny," she finished lamely.

Picard smiled uncomfortably.

"Susy, come on to the snack bar with me," he said, taking her arm lightly despite the other police. "We need some coffee, or a drink. I know how that guy can throw a scare into you."

"A drink," she agreed, knowing that there was none to

be had. The snack bar was closed. They walked to the canteen alcove and got two cups of coffee from the machine.

Picard led her to the elevator. The comfortable second-floor lounge was empty and Susy settled down on a couch with a sigh.

Picard eased himself down beside her and leaned back gently as she put her head on his shoulder.

"They told me when I got here you didn't get him." She paused and said intensely, "I wish you had, got him and killed him."

He glanced at her, but she was staring into the semidark room. There was no humor in her voice now. Something in it, the character of the intensity, alarmed him.

"He is evil, evil. I can't tell you how evil. I wish it had been you there. Because then you could know ..." The note was in her voice again, one Picard had never heard there before, one almost irrational. The man's strength had terrified him, but he had rallied. What had Paulier done to Susy?

"C'mon, Susy," he said gently. "Just give us the facts, ma'am, like the television cops." She snuggled closer and breathed a deep breath.

"Well, he must have come from beside the hedge," she began, carefully controlling herself. "But I hadn't seen him when I passed there before. I got to the shadowy part and ... and there he was right in front of me."

She leaned forward, away from him, and reached for her coffee on the low table before the couch. She took two or three swallows.

"I don't know that he said a thing. He smelled strange, I noticed that right away, not rotten like you and Roticella said, more complicated, like an apple that the wasps are flying around, musty, but autumny ... I can't explain. But he hissed, and those awful red eyes, like red fire, coals. God, they were anything but dead the way they are in his picture. I could see the iris was dark brown, almost black, and the whites were bloodshot lines. . . . The lashes were thick, and Harry, I just can't say this right, but the eyes, they weren't repulsive. Evil, evil, but not to turn you away. I . . . I couldn't stop looking at him. It was like some sort of spider sucking out all my juices. Destroying me right there on the sidewalk.

"And I felt I was going to faint, and I tried, I tried to break out of that stare of his, but I couldn't. He was drawing everything out of me—my job, that you were trying to trap him, even things about me, even personal things. Then . . . then he was gone.

"I was conscious of myself again, it was like I had been left hollow, worthless. I mean something of me went with him and the rest of me wanted to go with him. I'm ashamed, Harry, so ashamed . . ." She sobbed for a moment, then with difficulty regained her control.

"You see, he knew I was bait for him. That's why he turned away; but he marked me, and if it sounds crazy, well, I can't help it."

Picard was shaken by Susy's outpouring, with its hints of hysteria, like the emotional talk of an overstimulated child.

"Why don't you stay in the hospital for a night?" he said uncertainly. He had not thought that she could have been so shattered. She needed a sedative, and perhaps she would feel secure here.

"No," she said more calmly. "I've got to go home. There's the boy. And I want to." She turned to him and took one of his hands in both of hers.

"Harry, you don't think this all sounds too crazy, do you?"

He was bewildered. What she was saying was that Paulier in that instant they were together had read her mind. This he could not believe. But his liking for her made him

167

an accomplice in what he thought was her delusion.

"Baby, if you say it, then I have to go along with you," he said. "I know you're no psycho. If it hit you this hard, then it was something big."

"Well, that's it," she said, controlled. "My arm is bruised, he must have gripped it like a vise, but I didn't even notice." She stood up and took off her light coat. Then she pulled up her right sleeve and sat down, holding her right arm out to him.

Even in the soft light he could see the flesh marked with a vertical bruise where the fingers had bitten and a single mark where Paulier's thumb had gouged. Picard reached out and touched the bruises lightly.

Her features had just enough in them of the child who has been hurt, without knowing why, to make his heart go out.

"I bruise easy, Harry," she said, sadly humorous, looking at his eyes. He put his arm around her waist, and with his other hand he pushed her hair back from her ears. Then he kissed her deeply. She kissed him back firmly, giving herself up. He knew that he could have her right there, in the lounge. His mind thought of all that was needed. A quick latching of a door. But it should wait, could wait.

When he broke the long kiss she said:

"Stay with me tonight. . . ."

"Okay," he replied. And they rose to go.

They went back past the emergency-room desk and he called headquarters to check out. But the desk lieutenant transferred him to Pulanske.

How was Susy? asked the homicide captain. Fine, said Picard cautiously. Was he okay? asked Pulanske. Fine, Picard answered. He knew that the next question was the one that prompted the call—could he drop by headquarters on the way home? They would want to lay out the next day.

"Fine," said Picard despondently.

Susy looked upset when he told her that he must go to headquarters.

"I'm afraid, Harry," she said quietly.

"Then why not stay in the hospital until I'm through at headquarters?" he replied with some irritation, but she shook her head wearily. Then why didn't she come with him to headquarters?

"Oh no, I'm just being neurotically afraid. I'll go home now. How long will you be? An hour? No, I don't need any county policemen standing by." She buttoned the light coat and looked at him wistfully, a wrinkle of smile on her lips.

"One cop in the house will be too many tonight," she said.

She took her apartment key off its hook in her key wallet and gave it to him matter-of-factly.

"I'll use the one above the doorjamb," she said. "Don't knock. The boy sleeps like a rock, but the neighbors don't."

He waited with her in front of the hospital until a taxi came, then he kissed her briefly before he handed her in. Her concern made him feel uneasy. He was anxious to get back to her. Why? he asked himself. No, not just that, he answered himself. Why else? To guard her, he replied.

At headquarters Pulanske laid out the plans brusquely. He was angry that the man had escaped. He could be forgiven the first time, but now a trap that had been set up by him—in which night after night of surveillance had been invested—had snapped shut on its quarry. And unaccountably the victim had escaped.

The local businesses would be circularized with Paulier's picture. He would get an augmented night force put on in the precincts. The vice squad would be asked to exhaust every possible source of information in the whore-pimp underworld they dealt in. The man must have come in a taxi or else he parked his black Dodge nearby. He would tell the hack bureau to send out notices.

Picard was utterly discouraged. The killer had been cornered and had escaped.

It was 3 a.m. when Picard pulled in front of the square mass of apartments that included Susy's. He drove around the block looking for an open space among the backs of parked cars on the poorly lit streets.

There was a black Dodge. He caught his breath. A '60, a '61, too. But he sighed with relief. Maryland plates. Paulier had D.C. plates. God! Stolen plates! The thought hit him like a blow in the groin. He jerked his car to the opposite side of the street and swerved in beside a "No Parking" sign.

He ran to the car, felt with his hand the still-warm engine, and then wrenched open the door. The smell of the killer Paulier made him choke.

Crying aloud with fear for Susy, he began to run between the squat four-story buildings as fast as he could.

God, God, God, he thought, Paulier followed her home, but even in his anxiety he remembered what she said: "... drawing everything out of me." Had she told him somehow where she lived?

In the shadows between the two buildings he tripped over a low wire fence and fell sprawling, feeling his pant leg tear and a sharp scrape of skin from his shinbone. His hands hit hard, but it did not knock out his breath. He scrambled up, hurting vaguely all over, and ran on sobbing, God, God, in terror of what might even now be happening.

Picard ran up the stairs of Susy's apartment house, cautious enough to spring two steps at a time lightly and quietly until he reached her door. For an instant he paused, but the only sound was his heart beating fast and hard from his pent-in breath. Too late, he thought despairingly. Not a sound, not a sound. He had the key in his hand, and with one quick motion he put it in the lock and flung open the door, stepping aside a split second to pull the forty-five from its holster as he burst into the room.

At first he thought the man was raping her. The scene was too violent for any lesser crime. But her attacker actually was crouched like a huge black animal over her upper body. His arm and half of his right chest were thrown across her as she lay on the couch. The man—it was Paulier—snapped his head around without loosing his hold and Picard realized the full horror of the drama.

The bottom half of the man's face was covered with blood, and Picard could see past him where Susy's torn throat was bleeding freely.

Picard, with a groan in his chest, rushed at the man. He could not fire, as Susy was too close. But as the man rose Picard smashed him across the face with the pistol.

It should have felled him, and Picard was drawing back to strike again, when he felt that terrible grip on his forearm. The gun fell from his hand.

He swung with all his might with his left hand at the man's head. They were too close for Picard to get him in the face or to knee him. The fist met solid flesh but failed to stop Paulier, who spun the detective to the floor, knocking a lamp from the table. Before Picard could scramble up the man was on him.

The detective was a wiry man in good condition, but he knew he had no strength against this opponent. He clawed at his shirt for the gold cross, but had to thrust the man's huge foul head aside as it came toward his throat, the hideously long white teeth bared.

Picard rolled left and right as the man in black tried to pin him to the floor. The cross, the cross, he thought, but he could no longer free his arms. He smelled the nauseating stink that he had encountered in the barn, and just above him now he saw the red wild eyes with their brown-black centers.

At close range he felt the full force of Paulier's gasping and vile breath. The demon let go one arm, and Picard tried to thrust him clear, but Paulier brushed his arm aside and forced the detective's head back, arching Picard's throat as if preparing it for a butcher's ax. Picard felt the vomit rise chokingly even as the man opened his maw wide showing what looked like daggers of ivory where his canine teeth were.

This is it, Picard thought grimly.

But instead of the deadly bite that Picard knew was coming, indeed had almost experienced in his mind, the man looked up and suddenly uttered a hoarse shocked cry of alarm. He rolled off Picard like a huge cat and crouched above the vomiting detective for a moment.

Paulier expelled his breath with a guttural sound, an unforgettable combination of hatred and defiance and fear.

"I am not finished with you," he said to Picard in a voice hoarse and deep with enmity. Then he looked up past Picard again and, growling like an enraged wolf, he backed, half crouched, into Susy's bedroom.

Picard, still weak from the tumult, turned on his side, aware suddenly that his right arm was numb below the elbow, and looked back to where the man's eyes had focused. It was Mrs. Kearns, frozen like an ice statue, the hole of her mouth gaping. She stood stone silent, her hair tightly wrapped in curlers, one hand gripping her flannel nightgown, the other pressed to her heavy bosom.

And from that hand hung what she had no doubt snatched from under her pillow to protect her as she came to her young neighbor's aid—a black-beaded rosary.

The golden cross at its end—which had saved Picard

from Paulier seconds before—glistened as it swung with the fear that slightly swayed her body. The cross shone with its many rubbings in the subdued light of Susy's room.

Picard, knowing that his right arm was broken or badly injured, inched into Susy's bedroom and saw the window open wide where Paulier had fled. He crept back to where Susy lay, head and upper body still on the couch, right leg slipped off onto the floor, her blue dressing gown caught just above her knees.

"Get a doctor," he croaked to Mrs. Kearns, breaking the spell that had held her almost motionless. His voice startled her and she picked up the phone and dialed the operator. Picard dimly heard her speaking as he raised himself to look at Susy's throat. Gratefully he saw that although the blood was oozing it was not pumping from the great tear.

She was unconscious, but her breast rose and fell with breathing, steady breathing, trancelike, unlike the gasps that still shook the detective. It was the last thing his policeman's mind remembered before the pain from his arm and aching body came over him in a huge, brain-numbing wave, and he rode on it into unconsciousness.

Picard awoke and there was light outside his window. He knew that he was in the Hospital Center. But his mind was foggy. A doctor and Pulanske were in the room. He could not remember if he had asked about Susy, but Pulanske was saying something that sounded somewhat distant through the ring in his ears.

"Susy is going to pull through, Harry. I've got her kid out with my four boys. It all looks okay. We're fine, we're still working on the case. Now forget it, forget it."

Then he shut his eyes and let his anxious thoughts roll over him like gutter water over a pebble. He was done with it; this time he was sick, too sick to support thoughts of it, unable to act, if he had such thoughts, and glad at least for the time being to be done.

Once during the long day he awakened and remembered that he had been conscious when they set his arm. And was a rib broken? Here was tape on his right lower chest. His legs were bruised and his head ached. His stomach felt queasy. And at some time Pulanske had questioned him about the car. But now he was at peace.

The next morning, the May sunshine through his window, the soundless toy cars running along the thruway that passed the hospital, the city waking to work—these things gathered him back to the life he had briefly absconded.

The doctor looked surprised when Picard asked him of Susy, then replied that she was in Holy Cross Hospital and that he had heard she would pull through. As for Picard, a broken arm, a broken rib, a mild concussion, multiple bruises. Otherwise, the doctor had said, smiling, he was fine. It would mean a few days more in the hospital, then a good long week before he tried to do anything at work.

"Yes," said the doctor, "of course you can have the newspapers for the last two days."

The first edition of the *Star* after the attack showed Susy's picture, pretty, younger than she was, a blowup of the police personnel shot. At the bottom of the page was a smaller picture of himself, a mug shot.

"Victim . . ." it said under her picture. "Police hero . . ." under his. The paper was only yesterday's. Then he had been out only one day. He wondered how his presence at her apartment was explained, and read through the details of the hotel and attack scenes to find it.

Pulanske had been both inventive and discreet.

Deep in the *Star* story Picard found the paragraph:

"Capt. Pulanske said he ordered Picard to deliver a special tear-gas weapon to Mrs. Finnerton's home. Pulanske, commenting on the homicide detective's mission, said, "The weapon arrived too late. Fortunately the weapon bearer was on time.'" Picard chuckled wryly. He glanced at the *News* and the *Post* for that morning. There was little new—the search for Paulier stepped up and still more fear throughout the city. He shuffled painfully to the television set and turned on the morning news. The WMAL cast featured a filmed interview with Mrs. Kearns, who apparently had been far from reluctant to discuss the case. The day's lapse between the events and the interview with her had not hurt her sense of drama.

She was primped up in her best black suit and told, as she held her rosary to the camera, how "I held out my cross and he looked mad enough to spit, why he would surely have killed that poor man . . ."

Well, thought Picard, running his fingers over the chain that held his own crucifix, that part of it was certainly true enough. He would have been killed.

The television reporter lingered, obviously unable to resist, on the "vampire-like aspects of the attack . . . the Dracula-clad attacker . . . pseudovampirism, a rare psychotic condition . . . almost supernatural strength . . ."

There was a blip, and his own picture flashed upon the screen. It was the same mug shot, startling him with its youth. Picard thought the hastily snapped picture from years ago did not really do him justice. He didn't have those staring eyes.

". . . is recovering rapidly in the Washington Hospital Center, according to doctors."

Picard called headquarters and chatted briefly with the young homicide detective who was the only man in the supersquad room. There was nothing new. Picard, exhausted from even this small effort, went back to bed.

That afternoon he called the Holy Cross Hospital in

Silver Spring and got the pat answer from the information clerk: "Mrs. Finnerton is in satisfactory condition. She is resting quietly. No, she cannot take calls yet."

The detective called the administrator's office and identified himself. The secretary said peevishly, "It's you people who told us to give no information on that patient without a call-back. What is your number, please?" The call-back came. The administrator, once he had linked Picard to the Department, was eager enough to talk: "Yes, that's right, heavy sedation," the doctor replied to Picard's questioning. "We had to begin when she came out of surgery. Well, the anesthetic was general and when she came out she was a bit hysterical . . . No, no screams, more whimpering, if you know what I mean . . . The surgery? Well, sutures of course and several pints of blood. I don't know how many. The jugular was pierced and partially, just a little, ruptured, but not sufficiently to be fatal, thank goodness. Oh yes, successful. Yes, indeed. No trouble anticipated at all physically . . . Well, that's what the heavy sedation is for, you see. She hasn't had any really lucid moments yet, but when she's conscious she's very anxious, very. This was a terrible shock to her whole system."

Picard cradled the telephone and leaned back in the bed. There was nothing, nothing he could do. Tomorrow he would talk with Pulanske. Not tonight. Softly the day outside was making a slow spring change through dusk to dark. The thought of night brought with it a general, unspecific ill ease. Picard had not encountered the feeling before. Thus he did not recognize it as simple fear.

Next day his doctor reluctantly let him check out of the hospital on his promise to rest. He caught a cab to Holy Cross Hospital. The young doctor on duty would not let him question Susy. ("I thought we made that clear to Captain Pulanske.")

Picard said that he would visit her as a friend. Only

then did the young doctor—cutting short his little talk on visiting hours—put the name "Picard" together with the cast on his arm.

"Oh, you're the detective who fought . . ." he began, his doctor's superiority dropping away before the newspaper hero. Picard looked at him coldly. He did not like most doctors, only those from the city's emergency rooms, with whom he joked and talked shop after they had labored hard and sometimes successfully to save the shooting and knifing victims they both served.

This new suburban doctor in his new suburban hospital had seldom handled the violent, human manglings that were treated nightly at the municipal hospitals.

The young doctor deferred to him and let him go into Susy's room.

She was asleep in the antiseptic room and he did not wake her. Bandages were on her throat, giving her, like the nuns who served in the hospital, the chaste look of a member of a religious order.

Her face, free of make-up, was pale, a little thin. But for its good profile, its good bones, it would have been a tired, unattractive face. Her lips were slightly apart. The lashes lay long on her cheeks, her hair was brushed close to her head.

Picard regarded her dispassionately. She was so still. His gaze was unaffected by the objective fact that he loved her.

"You'll tell us, I guess, when she comes around," he said to the doctor.

"Yes," said the man in a stilted way, aware that the detective did not like him and why.

Picard went home and read a mystery story. When evening came he called Pulanske. There was no news. Yes, the chief had him on the carpet.

"I told him we're trying to fight a goddamn superman," said Pulanske. "He said he was getting calls from Capitol

Hill saying 'How come?' I told him to be grateful there were no more bodies."

Picard grunted glumly.

"Harry, it's going to take a new set of rules to catch this nut, a whole new set. And remember, the FBI isn't doing a damned bit better on it than we are."

That night Picard dropped in at A.V. Ristorante for a late supper and found himself a table near the rear with enough light to read the final of the *Star*. He did not want to be alone in the apartment.

Mario, the owner, came and sat down with him for a glass of the Orvieto he served to his friends.

"You got vampire problems, Harry?" he said.

"You bet, Mario. At least we got a guy that thinks he's one."

The thought of the man's iron grip made Picard reach for the little cross inside his shirt. He found it and pulled it out. It shone in his hand.

"I never even thought I was a Christian," he said with a rueful smile, remembering that he had not been to a service except for funerals and friends' weddings since he was a boy.

"You ever think of wearing one of these for protection?" he said to the lean restaurant man.

"Harry, I been wearing one for protection all my life," said Mario, pouring the two of them glasses of wine.

Within a few days Picard felt almost well. He had mastered one-armed driving and drove easily through town toward the hospital. The clouds were gone. The sky was a light cerulean blue that seemed made to order to float above and around Washington's marble monuments and memorials, to brighten the stern phony façades of the government buildings.

Driving through the park, he felt the cool close in. The

green was fresh, the city air purified there among the old trees.

Susy was stronger, the hospital told him. She talked quite coherently, although she was still being fed intravenously. The damage to her throat had left her with little desire to swallow, and in any case she appeared to have no wish to eat.

Two nuns were in the waiting room, looking crisp and new in their habits, a pair of tulips. Behind them was the somber figure of Christ on his cross. Smaller ones were in every room.

Paulier would not venture here, Picard mused.

Picard followed one of the nuns to Susy's room. He was heartened to see Susy's face fuller, less pale. He sat near her bed. The nun left them with a cautionary look at the detective. "Do not upset her," the look said.

The policewoman smiled weakly.

"You look wonderful, much better," he said awkwardly.

Her throat was lightly bandaged now. She wore a pale yellow short-sleeved bed jacket. She was gently propped up and her round arms lay easily by her side.

"Thank you, sir," she said huskily.

"I saw the boy," he started. "He said, 'Where the hell's my mother?' Pulanske is turning him into a foul-mouthed little cop."

"That's not true, he didn't say it," she said, smiling.

"No," said Picard. She's better, he thought, but still how fragile.

"You don't have to say funny things for me, Harry," she whispered, looking into his eyes. She moved her arm toward him with some effort and he put his hand over hers.

"That feels good," he said.

She nodded her head slightly, her eyes grateful. Then the tears came up into her eyes and ran down her cheeks.

He pulled a Kleenex from a box on her table and blotted them. She cried in soft little sighs and the tears kept welling up. He leaned toward her.

"Susy, Susy. We'll make it come right." She wept a moment longer, then said, "Give me a Kleenex."

He put one in her hand. She blew her nose and looked up, red-eyed now.

"I'm going to be all right," she said, closing her eyes. When she opened them, he saw that she was tired.

"Come see me, come tomorrow," she said, her hand moving slightly until he reached down and took it again. Picard left the hospital, wondering if anyone could make it right.

At the office, he worked on the futile, continuing leads. And his arm slowly healed.

He visited her almost daily. But she did not turn to the night she was injured, nor did he press her.

Finally she came to grips with Paulier's attack on her.

"I should want to get out of here," she told him. Her voice was stronger, but she still had no desire for food and the pallor clung to her.

Picard smiled uncomfortably.

"The psychiatrist here says I have to make up my own mind. He's been coming every day. He's very helpful, you should try one."

"I got no problems, Susy," he said.

He reached for her hand and she gave it willingly. It was a familiar gesture for them. She rubbed his thumb lightly, then went on. But he had felt her grip tighten.

"Harry, let me tell you about it. I can think about it sometimes and other times I have to force my mind away. I can feel myself toppling off the wire, toward hysteria." She smiled quickly at him.

"When you left me that night I was shaky, still shaky,

you remember. But the cab took me home and I checked my boy and he was all right.

"I got into the dressing gown." She stopped for a moment.

"I felt like if I were going to be a *femme fatale* with you, why, I might as well do it right. And I hadn't played the *femme fatale* for a long time," she said with a small rueful look.

She cleared her throat as her voice hoarsened slightly. He poured her a glass of water and she took a sip, then reached again for his hand.

"I had on that little cross you gave me. But the chain, it seemed to feel strange, uncomfortable on my neck, so I took it off. I sat on the couch, working on my nails. I felt, heard, I guess, a sound back by my bedroom door . . ." She caught her breath sharply and said in a weak, quick voice:

"There he was. . . . You may think I would have screamed," she said, speaking more rapidly, her tone more agitated. She gripped his hand tightly. "And that's part of the problem, but it was like a dream when you try to scream, except, Harry, part of me didn't want to scream at all, not at all.

"He was looking at me with those dreadful eyes, dead at first and then they were red, not really but dark brown. And then I knew he had me hypnotized or whatever that feeling is, like fainting. Only a tiny part of me was aware of what was going on. This was the only me, the only good me."

He looked down at their clasped hands. Her knuckles were whitening from her grip, as if this pressure would ensure the rest of the story coming out, would keep up the flow of words. Her face was moist.

"Harry, I don't know whether I talked to him or whether he just read my mind, consumed my mind again. But I told him everything, gave him everything, me, all about the case . . . about the prostitute Sophie, the professor, and about the Scandian girl. He seemed to be questioning me . . ."

She stopped again. Her breast rose and fell with abnormal excitement. He could feel her trembling toward hysteria. Picard tried to hush her.

"That's enough Susy, nuff, nuff."

"No, no, I just want to say this," she gasped, on the brink of incoherence. "His eyes, his face, it's not ugly, and I know if I go back that he'll come and get some more of me . . . Even when he has drained all I know . . . and when he . . . God, God, he came at me, at my throat, and even then, I couldn't stop him, didn't want to, even when I felt his mouth . . ."

She reached to her throat, where her hands fluttered. Her eyes, clear and cornflower blue when they had been so serene a few minutes ago, were stark and tormented. Suddenly she buckled toward him from her propped position, sobbing. He caught her and she wept into his chest.

"And the worst thing . . . the worst thing . . . is that I want to see him again . . . Harry, he wanted me to take that cross off, and I did, and I've felt him wanting me now, even now, with blessed Jesus over my bed . . ."

He held her until the sobs ended. She turned her head from where it was buried in his chest and without leaving him wiped her face with tissues he gave her. Then, her face streaked and miserable, she looked at him.

"God, you poor booby, stuck with a hysterical woman."

"What a mess, what a mess," he groaned. Her emotional release also freed him to say what he felt, honestly, tactlessly.

Picard's doubts that began when she had broken down after Paulier's encounter with her at the hotel returned. He knew that it had been a terrible effort for her to talk just now of what had happened. He wanted to understand.

But he had been a bachelor for a long time, and he was cautious. "Suppose you wind up with some kind of kook on your hands," a self-protective voice told him.

On the next day she took her first trip outside the hospital. He left the afternoon trick at 4 p.m. and picked up her son at Pulanske's house. The boy, who had seen her only twice since she was injured, was shy when he walked into her room. Then she showed him a crayon sketch of brightly colored houses and dogs she had drawn for him. The two chattered excitedly and, seeing the love she had for her son, Picard wondered how any wall could grow between himself and her.

She dressed in a yellow linen suit while he and the boy waited in the lobby. The three of them drove along the Maryland section of Rock Creek for an hour, and then returned.

They left her in the hospital waiting room. Picard watched her, still a little hesitant on the heels, but so excellent in leg, in waist, in shoulder, and in carriage of head, as she walked down the corridor toward her room. He thought to himself that he wanted her whether she ever got well or not.

Next morning, De Perugia, of the vice squad, dropped down from the fifth floor and walked into the supersquad room, where he sat on Picard's desk. The homicide detective looked up sharply but hopefully at the vice man. He quickly read the message on De Perugia's plump face: no news.

"No, I got nothing for you, Harry. They are all scared, the bimbos. They've even stopped hustling anything but fat, pale guys with Southern accents and blond hair. None of them tall, dark, and handsome foreigners, not for love or money . . ."

Picard looked back down and almost aimlessly pushed

at the morning mail, the letters from other city police departments with their missing-persons reports, crank notes, inquiries, all to be read, gleaned for a single kernel of a clue.

He still wore a light cast, but could use his arm sparingly. When he checked that day with the police surgeon, the physician showed him the X-rays and painstakingly explained why his arm would never be as strong as it was once, what with the two consecutive breaks. Picard nodded stoically. He had never thought he would get through his police career without a scar.

Saturday afternoon he helped Susy move back into her apartment. The hospital had cleared her physically. And the psychiatrists, with some reservations, had helped her decide that she could trust herself to go home.

Mrs. Kearns had agreed to move in with Susy at night and help out during the day until Susy regained all her strength.

Bernard, Susy's son, was timid as he went in the apartment. Then the child informed them carefully that he wanted brothers like the Pulanske boys. Bernard lauded the life at the homicide captain's home until Susy said to him with a pale smile that, well, maybe they should pack up his things and let him go back there.

The youngster looked doubtful for only a moment, then ran to his mother and scrambled into her arms. No, he told her, he would stay with her.

The widow Kearns had placed several large crosses in each room. Susy led Picard into her bedroom, where the windows opened to the warm air of late spring. On the sill was firmly tacked a long string of garlic like a miniature tank trap.

Picard looked at the neat dressers, the smartly made bed. Behind the pillow were two more strings of garlic. The room combined the farmers market smell of the herb bulbs with the feminine smell of good perfume. Picard found the mixture oddly exciting. Susy turned to him.

"I don't even like garlic except in salad and salami," she said, smiling sadly.

He laughed and drew her to him, kissing her gently on the lips. She kissed back warmly, then her lips quivered and she retreated into the living room, where the boy played with the plastic autos Picard had brought him, all unaware of the grownups' complicated world.

Picard worked hard and fruitlessly during the next week. At night he generally visited Susy. Sometimes he found her bright, as on the day he brought her to the apartment. But other times she was tense and withdrawn, as if she waited uncomfortably for something she would not welcome.

One day she said to him, "I can't help it, Harry. It was too much for me. I don't think I'll ever feel well until he's gone. It's like an open wound."

And Picard knew this was true.

Sebastian Paulier, who had struck fatally and—in a criminal sense—classically so many times, hit a glancing blow early on a June morning in a run-down little street called Corcoran. A woman, insomniac and old, heard a child's scream through her open third-floor window and waddled from the bed to look out. Below her, in the half light that grayly illuminates the city's east-west streets while the great north-south avenues are still dark, she saw what she could scarcely believe.

A man in black, his suit coat flapping on his long body, sought vainly to stoop and snatch up a wriggling child clad in what appeared in the predawn to be pajamas. The child's frantic screams pierced up to her again, and she cried out:

"Let her go, police, help!"

The tall man swooped again at the child—a girl, three or perhaps four—and caught her arm as a car rounded the corner. The auto lights suddenly flicked from driving to upper beams. They spotlighted the grotesque drama, and the man in black, as if hit full by a burst of sunlight, threw both arms before his face. The child shrieked in pain as he released his grip on her. The car accelerated and screeched to a halt not fifteen feet from the man and the freed child.

The old woman watched as the man turned and broke into an oddly stiff but swift run down the sidewalk. From the car two husky youths tumbled out. With quick glances at the screaming child, they clattered down the sidewalk after the fleeing man.

Now, fearing for the child, the old woman rushed down the stairs in her housecoat. The little girl sat, terrified and howling, in the gutter, and she scooped up the child with a great sigh, seeing the bruises already rising on the arms and cheeks.

She ran inside, her throat constricting, and panted up the three flights of stairs, the child in her arms, bumping and pressing her knees as she climbed. Safe in her room with the whimpering child, she called the police.

The two men who had chased the marauder lost him in a twisting alley behind Corcoran Street, but their description was enough to prompt the precinct to call in Picard almost immediately. The child was no help. Some realization of the fearful fate she had escaped registered on even her unsophisticated mind. Picard dared not show her Paulier's picture for fear of making her hysterical.

She was reunited with her parents after they showed up in a panic at the precinct house at eight o'clock. The window to their daughter's room was open, the bed empty—and their first hopes that the child had simply crept out on the second-floor fire escape were quickly dashed. The abductor apparently had crept up the escape ladder and noiselessly stolen the sleeping child, only to have her wriggle free a block away.

"Teef, teef," the little girl had finally squeaked when the parents had soothed her and asked her how the kidnaper looked, but there were no tooth marks on her, only the bruises.

Picard called Pulanske at home and detailed the morning's events. Pulanske's voice carried the vigor of the hunt in it.

"Harry, he's holed up around there. He was taking the kid home, my God, to bleed her, I guess. This is the first time he's fluffed one."

Homicide and precinct detectives immediately began the long ordeal of questioning everyone in the block. The street had its share of crime and criminals. The residents, from long experience, were wary. Talking could mean long waits at court and serious reprisals from the friends of defendants.

The officers made slow progress. They found a man who thought he had heard a scream, but "That ain't the first scream I ever heard 'bout dawn on this street, no sir."

Two of the houses in the block were condemned, a third was vacant, and one was being remodeled by an optimistic bookstore owner from Georgetown who believed that any house with a flat face could be converted into a town house.

By evening the house-to-house check was completed for the block, and half of the next one, and nothing of value had been found. Picard expected nothing. Surely Paulier would be miles away by now. But, anxious to press every possibility, he obtained the precinct captain's promise that a man and his K-9 would patrol Corcoran Street that night. The officer would call Picard from the police box on the corner if anything happened.

The homicide sergeant was too tired to drive to Silver Spring that night, and settled for a call to Susy. Then he went to bed early.

That night he had another nightmare, his second since the case began. He dreamed that he was in the bed but was compelled to go to the door, although not to answer any knock. When he got there, he swung it open and there was no light in the hall, nothing but blackness. The blackness had substance, but no form. It had some sort of brooding life that was malignly gathering itself to encircle him. He began to gag for breath as the telephone rang him into wakefulness.

When he picked up the receiver, he was still gasping.

He looked at his watch and saw that it was just after 3 a.m. Four hours of sleep, he thought as he pawed at the phone table for a pack of cigarettes.

It was the patrolman on Corcoran Street. He felt a little silly, he said, but he thought, probably mistakenly, that he saw someone go into one of the condemned and abandoned dwellings.

Picard's dream-shocked mind came alert.

The house was in the middle of the block, between the street lights, said the policeman. He was certain that he had seen a man slinking up the stairway to the door. Then the man disappeared into the house, he thought. When he walked over he found there was a front-door alcove, all right, but the door itself was nailed shut and boarded over. . . . No, he hadn't tried to force it. He had gone to his call box and called the scout car and then Picard. Noise? No, he'd made none, but his damned dog had set to whining and had balked at going up the step to test the front door. Picard thought quickly of the dog at the farm and the sudden fate of the bloodhound, Buster.

"Tell 'em to keep the place under surveillance but to stay the hell away from it until I get there," he ordered. "Keep an eye on the door, but don't go near. Make sure they keep the scout cars around the corner, and no sirens, huh? And give a call to headquarters," he added.

Picard dressed hastily and strapped on his pistol. He fingered the gold cross about his neck. From the top drawer of his dresser he took a heavy brass cross about eight inches long.

This kind of blackjack the bastard understands, he thought, simultaneously reverent and irreverent. From the dresser he also gingerly took a small container with a cross embossed on its screw-on top. It was a vessel for holy oils that he had bought in a religious supply store. Priests used such containers on the way to administer extreme unction. Picard, feeling foolish but determined, had scooped it half full of holy water from a font in a Catholic church near headquarters.

Armed with the heavy forty-five, the cross, which weighed down his pocket, and his little vessel of water, he left the apartment. Funny, he thought grimly as he waited for the elevator to reach the ground floor, funny that he had more faith in the cross and phial now than he did the service automatic. But then he had seen the effect of the cross on the violently unbalanced mind of the murderer.

Picard ignored lights and speed limits as he crossed the wide but darkened avenues and sped toward Corcoran Street. I know how the bastard operates, he thought to himself. He is not working against a rookie now. He has broken my arm and has learned some of our weaknesses, but I have learned some of his. It is a little fairer now, he thought with a calm eagerness.

It was two hours at least until dawn. Picard wondered what really would happen to the killer if he got a dose of sunlight. Nothing? Or would he crack up? Vampires in the old stories reverted to the form they would have had if they had deteriorated like ordinary corpses. And for Paulier? Dust? Was Paulier that old?

"Stupid thoughts," said Picard aloud. Paulier probably

was abroad every day in some perfectly ordinary guise, a Dr. Jekyll and Mr. Hyde sort of nut, he thought.

He pulled up short behind a silent row of police cars. Their lights were out and the only sound he could hear was the low, mechanical challenge and response of the police radios in the line of cars—a chorus of sorts.

A uniformed lieutenant from the precinct got out of his car and walked to Picard. Up ahead, Robley unfolded from a headquarters car. Picard gripped the lanky detective's arm to let him know he was glad to have a veteran of their previous encounters.

"Lieutenant," he said softly to the precinct official. "We want to surround that house and I'd like you and some of your older men to go in with me. After we're in there's no reason why the cars can't move into the street. We'll want some radio communication right out in front."

He looked at the grizzled old lieutenant, then said slowly: "You may think this sounds funny, but I'd suggest the men that come inside carry crucifixes. If they aren't Catholics, they can borrow them from the rookies here who are. And the men who surround the place should have them, or just a pair of crossed sticks handy. We'll want to bunch this guy in to the center or up against a wall if he breaks loose. . . ."

Picard loosened his tie and opened his collar. He fished the cross from around his neck.

"If you don't have one take this," Picard said.

The lieutenant was staring at him as if he were crazy.

"Crosses?" he gasped. "Do you guys believe that stuff?"

Robley turned to the uniformed official.

"Lieutenant, I've seen the way this nut is frightened by crosses. Me, I haven't been in a church since I was old enough to skip, but I damned well got one."

He pulled a cross on a rosary from his coat pocket.

"And I got Father Brennan to say some abracadabra

over it, too," he said. The lieutenant took Picard's cross and smiled crookedly.

"I'm the only Rosenbaum in a couple hundred generations to ever carry one of these things, I guess," he said.

Picard tightened the top of his holy-water vessel, and he and Robley walked silently down the dark street on the side of the house, close into the shadows from the building. In the back the lieutenant had posted men in the jungle of ash cans, old board fences, and junk which walled in the rear of the condemned three-story house. The rear door was nailed shut and also partially boarded over. There was no rear cellar door leading up from the subsurface basement.

Robley groaned softly as one of the uniformed patrolmen turned his ankle in the dark and cursed. Behind them a half-dozen men followed single file in the shadows. Robley crept forward closer to the front steps, then motioned them back deep into the shadows with the crowbar he had brought for forcing the door.

From the sidewalk Robley and Picard could see the weathered boards on the front windows and the broken glass in the second- and third-floor windows. The old iron steps sprang from the bricks, and near their juncture with the house was a cast-iron coal-chute cover. The two detectives tiptoed up the steps. They glanced at the chute cover, set into the bricks and as large as a cellar window.

Crisscrossed boards nailed the front door shut. Picard felt for the big nails that sealed it.

"Nobody got in here," he whispered.

"The coal chute underneath?" asked Robley.

"It'd take some wriggling," was the reply.

Picard moved out of the alcove and Robley crowded in. The general assignment man worked the prongs of the crowbar between door and frame near the lock. He gave a wrench. The first effort brought a splintering sound as some of the old wood in the door broke loose. But Robley expertly inserted the crowbar again. This time the door and the boards across it shrieked and pulled free of the frame. The lock snapped clear of the latch plate. Robley jerked the door wide open and growled, "Watch the nails," as he darted in, hugging the wall.

It was pitch black inside. The house smelled stale with old paper and plaster. The policemen stirred up a small, irritating cloud of dust as they shuffled in. Robley and Picard caught their breath for a moment to listen. They heard nothing.

Robley, holding his flashlight far out to the side of his body, flicked it on and off once. It showed stairs leading to the second floor and a wide arch opening from the front hall into another room. Robley, with Picard directly behind him, sprang into the arch and again flashed his light on the stairs, then flicked it off. The two detectives heard the next two raiders scramble into the house and head up the stairs. One slipped, grunted without cursing, and hurried on up.

Picard and Robley, never moving far from each other, flicked lights across walls and doorways for instants at a time, lest they provide more than a momentary target for a sally by Paulier.

The two detectives coughed as they scurried like huge earnest rats from room to dusty room, and finally into the kitchen.

Wires hung from fixtureless electricity outlets; old pipes stood out from the wall where a stove had been removed; the open doors of cupboards showed a caved-in box of baking soda and crumpled paper towels far back against the wall.

Picard flung open a small closet, then instinctively stepped aside as a heavy wooden ironing board whooshed out, past where it should have braced itself for ironing, and onto the floor like a severed tree limb. In a hallway next to the kitchen Picard opened a door and flashed his light into the blackness. It was the cellar stairs.

"Tell 'em we're going down, Robbie," whispered Picard to his partner. Robley hurried back and hissed the message upward even as the second-floor team started down, their floor searched.

Robley was back at the cellar stairs in a moment. Picard flashed a light downward and they saw a litter of old boxes, oil cans, a crippled straight-back chair, and a cheap cardboard wastepaper basket upside down.

With flashlights off, Picard led the way down the stairs, which ran beside the brick foundation of the house. At the bottom he tripped, cursed silently, then flashed the light around the basement. It was full of trash, the collected clutter of many years. By one wall ancient newspapers moldered in slipping piles. A garbage can festered putridly.

He heard a scuttle and shot his flashlight toward a stack of thin laths and plasterboard. A small plume of dust and the continuing vibration of the laths told him that a big rat was still fleeing the interlopers.

Toward the front of the cellar a divider made of thick, rough boards stretched from floor to ceiling. A door hung half shut, its spring dangling uselessly. Picard stepped through the trash toward the door, his nostrils and eyes filling with the dust of the years.

He swung the old door open. It gave more readily than he expected. He stepped inside, darting his light in quick flashes. As he caught his breath he smelled the smell. He felt a catch in his chest so sharp that it made him momentarily dizzy.

"Robbie," he whispered. "He's in here."

The two detectives stood with their backs to the wooden partition, facing a room as big as the one they had just left. With guns drawn, they flashed the lights at the old coal furnace, its drooping doors gaping open.

In the corner, beneath a stack of nail-studded boards, Picard saw a gleam of black.

"What's under there?" he whispered to his companion, snatching at his sleeve. The two men, not bothering now to flash their lights on and off, fixed the boards with a steady beam. They could see beneath the haphazard crate wood a long oblong object with an exposed light-steel corner.

Robley threw a packing case aside and the two men saw a large trunk, similar to the one in the barn but more modern.

"He's in there, Harry," said Robley, standing back warily. Robley reached forward to shove another case end from the lower part of the trunk. Picard came forward and with his flashlight hand pulled gently at one of the lifting straps of the trunk. To his surprise the trunk moved easily. It was apparently empty.

In seconds the two men pulled it to the center of the floor, and Robley, working with the heavy blunt screwdriver he pulled from his inside coat pocket, neatly snapped the hasp. He flung it open and the stink of the grave flooded the room.

"Empty, empty," Picard choked as he shot a beam into the lined trunk.

"No," said Robley. He muffled his nose with his gun arm against the smell and gently lifted the satiny lining to show dark stains: blood. "He kept them in here, the bodies, until he finished with them and got rid of them, Harry. Now maybe he's planning to use it to take off with again—"

As Picard reached to touch the stains, he heard behind him a sifting sound. He wheeled and saw an aperture by the furnace perhaps three feet high and two and a half feet wide. It was partially covered by a worn shield of wood.

"It's a coalbin; there's a rat in there," said Robley, but even as he spoke, the coal slid again and he knew that it was something bigger than a rat.

The two men hopped over the debris to the hole in the wall. It was toward the front of the house. Apparently the coalbin stretched deep under the sidewalk.

Picard dashed the shield out of the aperture and shined his light in. As he did, the coal, sloping up to about four feet in parts of the bin, shifted rapidly.

A corner of black wood, burnished brightly, shone through a mound of coal in the center of the bin. It was part of a huge box, and as they watched they saw the lid of the box begin to rise, raining coal as it did.

"Come out! You son of a bitch," said Robley excitedly, smelling clearly the characteristic stink of corruption they both had come to identify with the killer.

Picard and Robley held their forty-fives steady, both men gripping their guns tightly in preparation for a shot at the head. They fixed the beams of their lights on the widening space between the lid and the long box. Picard, for a moment, dropped his pistol to his side to feel with a thumb the reassuring bulk of the cross in his pocket.

It was as if the scene were played in slow motion, for the lid rose slowly, steadily, pushed upward by a black-clad arm. Then, to the horror of the two detectives, the face of Paulier rose from within as if he were doing an infinitely careful sit-up.

The full light of their flashlights hit his face and the two men saw it was as ghastly white as his shirt front. His cheeks began to fleck with coal dust even as they watched. The eyes that had been so fiery in the past were dull and glazed like those of a man deeply under a narcotic drug. He stared at, or rather past, them, without a change in the profoundly lethargic expression. His face, bloated and so pale except for the blub lips, was drastically unlike that of the lean murderer Picard had grappled with at Susy's.

Picard's first thought was that Paulier had suffered a mortal wound. Was he surrendering? His heart beat fast.

They had him, they had him, he thought, for it was obvious that the man was as calm as clay. Then it clicked in his head. Paulier, even as the vampires he imitated, had sated himself on blood and was trying now—desperately perhaps—behind the mask of quietness to rouse his powers from the deep sleep of the glutton.

"C'mon out, Paulier, and you won't get hurt," Picard said quietly, ready to fire at the man's unprotected head if he made any precipitous move.

But neither he nor Robley was prepared for the suddenness of the man's recovery.

Even as Picard saw him blink, the body of the man in black went tense. The hand gripped the top it had been slowly raising. The two detectives fired as one, the shots sounding hollow and stifled but tremendously loud. Before they could fire a second time, they heard a monster's growl of anger. Paulier flung the lid at them and it struck the wall inside the bin, blocking for a moment the entrance, where they crouched.

As the lid fell away from the entrance to the floor, the detectives again caught Paulier in their beams, a dark lanky figure leaving the box. Picard saw that it was a cheap unlined coffin. He fired at the man's head as it bobbed past his beam. But Paulier threw himself against the wall, just around the corner from where the detectives were. They could hear him gasping for breath inside the bin, perhaps only two feet away—but out of range. The coal dust made the detectives hack.

"Okay, Paulier, c'mon out," shouted Picard, aware now that trouble was certain. There was no answer, only the killer's heavy, fast breathing. The thump of feet sounded as the police on the floor above scurried toward the cellar door.

Paulier apparently heard them too. Inside the bin there was suddenly the screech of coal on the cement floor. Paulier had his footing and flung himself halfway out of the entranceway so violently that both detectives were tumbled to the floor. He scrambled to get the rest of his body out as the two men struggled with him.

Picard got his gun arm free but dared not shoot for fear of hitting Robley. He flipped his gun backward and wrenched at the heavy cross in his pocket. The detective squirmed awkwardly, thrusting the killer back toward the bin with one arm. Then his other arm came free; he cocked his arm with the cross in hand and brought it down massively on the gasping bulk of his assailant.

Paulier felt it hit his shoulder and recoiled. Picard drew back and swung again, missing Paulier, but the killer saw the cross and terror froze his efforts.

Picard twisted and saw the killer's face again, the black coal dust rimming the maw with its terrifyingly white teeth—the same face he had seen in the fight at Susy's. Frenzy seized the detective. With a huge effort he shrugged off the weight of the man in black.

"Back, back," Picard shouted hoarsely. He felt the man's bulk leave the tangle of their bodies. Paulier, panting guttural sounds of terror, retreated with the backward motion of a crab.

Picard swung the crucifix like a hatchet in a half circle and landed a glancing blow on Paulier's arm. Then the detective crouched firmly and prepared to swing again.

Paulier thrust his legs back into the aperture and struggled to work himself into the bin. But Picard clipped him solidly on the cheek, knocking him heavily to the floor. The terrified Paulier screamed as Picard had never heard a scream before: a high loud wail that began in his chest, rose to his lips, and then fell back into his throat with choking barks of pain.

"Hit him again, Harry," shouted Robley, who was flashing his light at the groggy popeyed face of the murderer. But Paulier, his mouth wide in agony, managed to roll away from another swing by Picard and scuttled on his back into the bin.

Behind Picard the other detectives were shouting encouragement, but the area was too confined for them to aid Robley and Picard. Picard, the feel of power in him, crawled into the bin after the withdrawing fiend, crying, "Surrender, surrender, surrender," as if the incantation would somehow force Paulier to obey. But the man in black had regained his self-possession.

As Picard started to rise upright in the bin, the man roared and shoved the coffin into Picard's shins, cutting him to the floor. Picard recovered his flashlight in time to see the man strike the coal-chute door with his naked fist. With his left hand, Paulier reached down and pulled a small old-fashioned satchel from the cavity where the bin narrowed and stretched under the sidewalk.

Picard tried to dislodge his own arm and hand from under the coal and the coffin. But before he could clear the crucifix from the coal, Paulier with a single stride left his place by the coal-chute door and kicked the coffin again into the wriggling detective.

The flashlight fell. The coal dust was thick. Picard, as he struggled to right himself, heard the coal-chute door ring loudly again. Robley slithered into the bin behind him and shot the beam of his light toward the chute door. It was open. The bin was quiet. Paulier was gone.

"Oh Christ," Picard sobbed between hacks. "He couldn't have got out. It's too small, too small." He flashed his light into the narrow section of the bin under the sidewalk, but there was no one.

Outside they heard shouts, then shots, and both detectives stumbled through the sliding coal pile to the chute door. Picard pulled himself up. There was a loud screech of tires, more shouts, and then nothing more. Picard dropped back down into the coal.

"They're after him," he muttered wearily. "The bastard got one of the cars." The two men, coughing and choking, crawled out of the bin into the cellar and hurried up the steps to the outside.

In the black street only the lieutenant's car was still before the house. A small crowd of neighbors, light housecoats protecting them from the morning air, watched from across the street.

Picard could hear on the police radio the chase of the car stolen by Paulier as the pursuit was quarterbacked by the communications center at headquarters. A dozen men were gathered around the car windows.

"What happened?" Picard asked the lieutenant, quietly and out of breath. The official first did not recognize him through the coal dust, then shrugged dejectedly.

"I hate to think about it," he said as he got out of the car. Standing with Picard, he spoke in a low voice.

"We heard this clang. It must've been the bastard hitting that coal-chute door. Well, we thought maybe you guys needed some help in there and we started up toward the front door.

"And, then before I could get ahold of things and get some of these kids in uniform lined up again, there was the second time he hit it, and believe me, Harry, I didn't even see him come out of the chute . . . and the next thing I know . . ."

He shook his head hopelessly.

"What do you mean the next thing you know?" said Picard, trying not to sound harsh.

"The next thing I see him behind the wheel of the cruiser. And off he goes with me getting in one or two shots. We did get two cars after him almost before he's around the corner."

Picard was disgusted by the grizzled lieutenant's ineptness, but he said only glumly:

"I don't guess he can get far in a police cruiser, even an unmarked one."

"He can tell who's after him by the radio," observed the lieutenant. Picard and the older man walked back to the cruiser.

He could hear that the tempo of the radio voices had decreased. Experience told him the pursuers had lost their quarry. Picard felt nauseous.

The homicide cruiser pulled up with the overnight crew and Robley and Picard left the gray-haired lieutenant to his investigation. The two homicide men in the front seat laughed at their colleague's coal dust face. Picard got in the back seat to smoke. Robley joined him and the radio voices droned on. . . .

"Scout 11, man with a gun, 1120 Webber Street . . .

"Scout 82, prowlers behind Alice Deal Junior High . . .

"Cruiser 92, Fourth Precinct wants you . . .

It was an old familiar chant, usually comforting for Picard, who heard the voices fanning out over the city as a warm strength, the tough, protective, even defensive cop voices. Now the drone, the absence of anxiety in the radio voices frustrated him.

A tenser voice came through, excited but controlled:

"All cars vicinity Sixteenth and Corcoran, the missing cruiser, black Chevy, J Q 428, now proceeding south on Sixteenth Street at U-Union, Northwest. Scout 131 is following him."

The driver of the homicide cruiser in which Picard sat lurched the car into gear and flicked on his siren as they pulled away from the abandoned house. He headed straight out Corcoran toward Sixteenth Street. They were almost at the broad avenue when Picard saw Paulier's stolen cruiser whisk by. A half block behind came the pursuing scout car, its red bubble top flashing. The homicide cruiser, kept in better shape than the scout car because

Pulanske used it himself, screamed out of Corcoran and accelerated after the two autos.

Picard was amazed. Why had the murderer reappeared so close to the scene five minutes after he had made good his escape? A Thirteenth Precinct car had picked him up only a few blocks north of the house. Did Paulier want his earth? No. Picard suspected that was what was in the valise. Vengeance? Curiosity? Not likely. Perhaps a shrewd maneuver to make it through downtown by the route closest to the house, where he would be least expected. But it had backfired. The alert precinct crew had spotted the unmarked car. Now for the chase.

The driver's partner in the homicide car snapped on his microphone and said, "Cruiser 21 here, we are one block behind Scout 131, which is behind the subject."

"Thank you, Cruiser 21," said the communications voice.

A block north of Scott Circle, on the periphery of the downtown area, they had gained on the scout car and were hitting eighty miles an hour. Picard could not see the stolen cruiser. It was running with no lights, the radio said. But he knew that when it reached the brightly lighted circle he would see it as it turned.

The scout car ahead roared down on Scott Circle. Picard gripped the seat side as he sensed catastrophe. Less than a half block ahead of the scout car he saw the stolen cruiser's rear end skid sickeningly as it turned left, the wrong way around the circle. For an instant Picard expected it to roll, but it wobbled level, regained its full forward motion, and roared on toward Massachusetts Avenue, a pathway toward the city's center.

The homicide driver braked hard and prepared to cut left. The scout car, however, had been going too fast to anticipate the surprise turn to the left.

"No, no . . ." Picard heard Robley mutter.

Picard watched in horror as the driver of the car ahead braked, then realized that this would throw him out of control, and tried to make the turn. The car began to spill on its side, but the frantic driver straightened the wheel and jammed on the brakes again as he reached the circle. Its speed was too great. The auto, its siren screaming and its bubble top flinging red light crazily, leaped the curb and plowed bucking across the shrubbery at the base of the circle's statue.

Picard heard the enormous impact of the fast-moving car as it rammed the base. Their own car touched the curb for a moment as it ripped left around the circle, recovered, and accelerated after the stolen car. Picard looked back to where the scout car containing the two uniformed men burned with leaping yellow flames at the base of the statue.

"Jesus," said Robley quietly.

"Scout 131 has crashed at Scott Circle. Get an ambulance and rescue squad down fast," said the man beside the driver into the microphone, his voice cracking. The man paused. "We are a block and a half behind the subject," he added quietly.

The four detectives were all but shattered by the collision that had surely dashed the life from two of their colleagues. But there was no time for such thoughts. The black car ahead of them flashed into the lights that flooded the entrance to the Thomas Circle underpass.

The stolen cruiser disappeared in the underpass, the homicide car close behind, then shot out of the other side. Picard reached for his holstered forty-five, but the pistol was missing. He had not picked it up from the floor of the cellar.

"Is it worth a shot, Harry?" said one of the men in the front seat, pulling his detective special from its holster.

"No, maybe not," Picard grunted, and the man reholstered his pistol.

Five blocks later, at Ninth Street, the stolen black cruiser cut hard right and Picard again gripped his seat for the lurch. He looked back as they rounded, and saw two more cars, one with a bubble top revolving, coming up fast. They too screamed around the curve in pursuit.

Down Ninth Street they tore, past the cheap hotels, the honky-tonk bars, the strip theater, and dime-a-look cooze shows, all dark except for small neon signs promising fun tomorrow.

At Ninth Street and broad Pennsylvania Avenue, two empty cruisers blocked off the street diagonally across from the FBI's building. Paulier swerved wide, one wheel jumping onto the sidewalk, and passed the auto barricade by inches.

Picard heard the crack of shots from the curbs as the detectives who had used their cars for blockades fired at the speeding stolen car. The homicide cruiser slowed and also passed the two cars.

Paulier's Chevrolet was taking the turns better, but the powerful homicide cruiser gained on the straightaways. Picard glanced momentarily to the left as they hurried on toward the Mall. The great, floating dome of the Capitol, lighted chastely by the moon, which was newly come from behind clouds, seemed to look down the greensward of the Mall at the race of tiny cars.

Unaccountably Paulier swerved right on Washington Drive in the Mall, then Picard realized that the killer feared another road block at wide Independence Avenue.

Paulier's black auto picked up speed in the narrow street, like a dark bullet rifling toward the giant shaft of the Washington Monument, directly in front of him. Then at Fourteenth Street he squealed into a left turn and roared toward the parallel bridges—one outbound, one inbound—spanning the Potomac. Looking back across the Mall, Picard thought that he could see a dozen cars strung out in pursuit, some with red lights flashing, and he could hear the whine of their sirens above the motor noise.

The radio communications crackled and came on:

"Attention cars pursuing stolen cruiser. Virginia police are blocking their end George Mason Bridge. Repeated, there will be a complete road block at Virginia end George Mason Bridge."

Picard cursed. The operator in his excitement had forgotten that the stolen cruiser had a radio. Near the Jefferson Memorial, Paulier's black cruiser screamed into a cutoff and up toward the inbound bridge. In order to avoid the road block the murderer was crossing the river going the wrong way and risking a crash with oncoming traffic.

The homicide cruiser's driver slowed and made the turn across the cutoff.

On the bridge the stolen cruiser sped at ninety miles an hour, hugging the left side of the span to avoid the dribble of oncoming cars. Paulier was obviously anxious to reach Virginia and its long stretches of unpoliced state roads before another barricade could be set up.

The homicide cruiser's radioman urged communications to speed the road block, but the spaghetti-work of turnoffs on the Virginia side could only hamper such a project.

Picard's cruiser also hugged the rail, but in front he saw the lights of a car coming straight down the same side directly toward Paulier's car. The speedometer bounced from ninety to ninety-five. Picard heard Robley gasp as he too saw the car coming.

The oncoming car swerved crazily as the driver saw Paulier's lightless sedan roaring toward him, but when he sought to get out of Paulier's path he caromed off a car beside him and was once more on a collision course. Picard gritted his teeth and gripped the back of the seat with one hand and the side with the other. The approaching car was hurtling directly toward Paulier's vehicle, when the killer swerved aside, missed the car, then straightened and sped on toward Virginia.

The lights of the oncoming car now blinded Picard as it came straight toward the four detectives. The homicide driver hit the brakes, but their cruiser skidded drunkenly and he let up; braking would only mean a swerve, then a long slide and death at the rail or in a crazy tumble into the rushing river below.

Then suddenly, as Picard shut his eyes and waited death, the car passed by them. Its driver had made a miraculous swerve to the center of the bridge. Picard looked out of the rear window and watched the heavy convertible try to right itself from the swerve. But it struck the rail on the other side of the bridge, careened across the street now completely out of control, and plowed through the retaining wall as if it were papier-mâché.

By the time the crash had registered on Picard's mind, the car and its driver had disappeared from the bridge and were plunging into the dark, high Potomac waters, leaving behind only the image of torn rails and gaping space between.

"Good Christ," uttered Picard.

Paulier had reckoned correctly. The Virginia police had one cruiser in the road at their end of the bridge, but the complex of cloverleaves had indeed prevented more from being transferred in time from the George Mason Bridge. The stolen cruiser's brakes shrieked again as Paulier turned down into an "up" ramp, bounced over a center strip, and cut into the George Washington Memorial Parkway, leading to the airport.

Picard braced himself and leaned over the front seat to where he could use the microphone handed him by the homicide detective.

"This is Picard in Cruiser 21," he said to the headquarters operator. "Get them to block the parkway at the airport. We are now close behind stolen cruiser. Repeat, get Virginia to block parkway at airport and force him into the airport area. Alert airport police to block their roadway at airport circle." He paused, then opened the mike again:

"Please advise airport police that subject is highly psychotic, highly dangerous. He is in extreme fear of crosses and other holy objects. Repeat, suggest all those seeking to subdue subject arm themselves with crosses. Subject is extremely psychotic and fears religious objects."

Picard wondered grimly what the madman in the car ahead would think when he heard that over the radio. Would he not fear an army of men with crosses? Would his diseased mind not snap soon from the pressures of this strange morning. Robley, in the back seat, laughed dryly.

"Harry, you know communications tapes all the messages. That sermon will make a nice little birthday gift for you, assuming we have any more."

The communications center was on again, repeating Picard's message for cars with only one-way reception. Picard heard muttering, then the voice of Pulanske.

"This is Pulanske. At the airport, try to encircle suspect and hold him at bay. We believe man is dressed in bulletproof material. Repeating, he fears crosses, is psychotic and fears crosses. Suggest if you need to fire, fire only at head or legs and at close range."

Picard was glad to have Pulanske in on it. In front of them, Picard could see the airport turnoff. The main highway was completely blocked with cruisers and an airport bus. Its yellow sides shone brightly in the lights. There was only one turn for Paulier, to the right toward the airport—and Paulier slowed and made it.

The string of pursuing police cars swerved off the main highway behind Paulier and accelerated as they recovered from the turn. The homicide cruiser was hard on the stolen car as it hurtled toward the airport circle, where, in front of the main airport building, Picard could see maintenance trucks and airport limousines forming a blockade to exit roads.

Suddenly a single spotlight stabbed its finger from the front of one of the waiting police cars into the windshield of the stolen cruiser. Paulier, apparently blinded, jammed on the car's brakes and the cruiser screeched and skidded up over the curb and onto the circle. It turned completely around on its four wheels and stopped.

Picard's cruiser slowed as it reached the circle, then the driver hit the brakes and brought it to a skidding stop. The car swung into the curb and Picard sprang out.

He saw the black figure of Paulier leap from his car and sprint in his stiff, precise run toward the terminal building. A small army of airport police, airlines personnel, and Virginia officers jumped from the shadows and from their cars in pursuit. Their lights and those of the cars crisscrossed. Their shouts sounded strange in the near dawn.

Two burly airport policemen, guns drawn and hunched like football tackles, blocked Paulier's way into the building. Paulier ran toward them, also crouched low. He held the valise cocked and ready to swing. The two men shot at almost point-blank range at the fugitive, but he continued on, swinging the bag out at them.

One of the policemen lunged beneath a swipe of the valise while the other grabbed at Paulier's upper body. But the killer brushed off their attack like a professional fullback running through a pair of school children. Picard was close behind, gripping the cross in his right hand. His arm had again begun to ache. He cursed the two airport men for endangering the lives of the pursuers with their futile shots.

The man in black swung through the doors and Picard

entered close behind. He could see others going through doors nearby, and he hoped there would be still more men inside to cut him off.

Paulier was obviously seeking to dash through the terminal and out on the runway. Why? To hijack a plane? Picard wondered as he panted into the waiting room. Not likely. To get to the river and escape? Perhaps.

At the end of the waiting room Picard saw a swarthy airline mechanic with a tiny object in one hand and a gigantic wrench in the other coming toward Paulier, but still twenty feet away. The stocky mechanic shouted something at the lanky figure and thrust up into the air what Picard saw was a tiny silver piece of metal on a thin chain, perhaps a cross or holy medal.

"Devil! Devil!" the short man cried. Paulier, who had veered to avoid him, threw up his arm in front of his face, hissing so loudly Picard could hear him.

The detective thrust his huge brass cross forward and cried between gasps, "Paulier, Paulier, look!"

The murderer turned at the familiar voice and started to lunge toward Picard when he saw the cross that had caused him so much agony earlier. He stopped short and stepped backward with that same expression of open and uncontrollable horror that Picard had first seen in the barn and again at Susy's apartment. Paulier dashed down the long wide lobby toward the restaurant, now dark, but Picard's delaying tactic had worked. Robley, his hair messed and sooty, his black stubble and determined eyes giving him the air of a fanatic monk, drove Paulier backing into the center of the lobby with his thrust-out cross of gold.

Paulier lunged toward steps leading to the airport gates, but an Alexandria detective, his crucifix still around his neck, the cross held forward between his thumb and forefinger, sidled bravely toward the enraged killer, crying, "Back, back, you bastard!"

The dead white face, streaked as it was with coal dust, rippled hideously with fear as Paulier saw the cross. He sprang back. His quick movements as he shuttled first toward one end of the lobby, then toward the other, were like those of a macabre folk dance or ritual—or some insane game of ring-around-the-rosy.

Thirty men now surrounded him, each with a cross or medal held out. They gave slightly as he rushed toward them, then moved back as he balked and shied at the religious objects.

Picard could hear him gasping deep in his throat. He moved forward toward the cornered killer and smelled the stink of corruption that he now knew so intimately. He gagged but rasped out:

"Surrender, Paulier. This is your last chance. Surrender!"

The fugitive turned toward Picard once again. The eyes that had been dead with sleep and satiety earlier now flamed red black with hate.

"You," said the venomous voice. "You ..." he growled with that animal sound that rumbled up from his chest. But in its tone now Picard recognized a note of anguish.

"Monster!" shouted Picard as Paulier swung the valise at his head. He thrust out the cross and at the same time he pulled from his pocket the little cylinder of holy water. With the container—the cross embossed on its cover—in one hand and the crucifix in the other he moved spiderlike toward the panting killer.

The man in black grunted at the sight. Then he whirled as he saw from the corner of his eye a man skulking up behind him with a gleaming bale hook poised to rip into his back. He downed the man with a flail of the valise.

"Paulier!" shouted Picard once more, twisting the top from his container with the hand that held the cross. Paulier turned again and the circle of pursuers closed expectantly. The fiend and his nemesis were face to face.

"Holy water," said Picard, his arm cocked with the container. "Holy water, Paulier."

The man at bay staggered backward at the words. His great white teeth struck together in terror, then his bulbous lips drew back from them in a frozen grimace. His chalky skin and the black dust combined with the shocked eyes and over-red lips to give his face a look of dread so intense it was like a pantomime of some satanic clown. But there was no scream. Only a huge expiration of breath.

The detective flung the water full in the madman's panic-stricken face, and the lobby seemed to shake with Paulier's wild animal scream. Picard saw the savage features writhe as the water mixed with the coal dust and ran down his face like acid.

Paulier screamed maniacally again and bowled through the circle of men, bounding toward the room-high glass windows that looked out toward the runways and the river beyond. With one last insane shriek, Paulier burst the glass with his valise, sending shards flying. The killer sought to step through the hole, but his pant leg snagged in broken glass and he dashed at the window again with his bag. As he swung the valise's handle gave and the old leather satchel flew back toward the lobby, opening as it hit a rail. Earth, Paulier's earth, scattered under the feet of the pursuers.

Paulier made an instinctive move back toward the earth. But Picard, shouting his name, rushed toward him with the empty water vessel. The killer, kicking another sheet of glass from the hole he had made, plowed through and tumbled himself over the parapet to the tarmac fourteen feet below.

Picard heard him hit with a thud, then looked out as Paulier clambered to his feet and ran to the left. Already a guard stationed on the outside was at him with his crucifix and Paulier turned back and limped to the right. A half-dozen detectives jostled down the stairs and on to the runway. Shouting his name, they thrust him back.

The hounded fugitive, blocked from any course but one, began to run swiftly toward the lights and sputtering engine flames of a plane on the runway nearest the Potomac. The detectives paced after him, picking him up with the flashlights as a grotesque of legs and coattails.

The man ran like the wind despite a heavy limp. He was outdistancing his pursuers when the siren of a scout car sounded. Its spotlight fixed Paulier thirty yards ahead and threw his shadow lengthily toward the river.

The patrol car, then another, shot past the fleeing man. Police bailed out and cut off his route to the river. The officers, brandishing crosses, succeeded in driving him back toward his hunters, who formed a loose semicircle as they ran after him. Paulier's steps, as he stumbled and twisted, seemed to falter in the gray light announcing dawn.

But as Picard drew near, Paulier broke through the line of detectives who had dismounted from the cars. Before him now was only the river, and across it the lights of the city, where the near dawn had dimly lighted the sky.

Only minutes stood between night and the first rays of the sun.

The motley army of airline workers and police was off after him again. Now he ran less fast. In the center of the pursuing groups several officers fired—no danger now of hitting their fellows.

Picard was all but out of breath. He could taste the cool, moist, slightly foul mist from the river. Paulier was limping badly and Picard saw him trip as he reached the rocky ground and the mudbanks that bordered the agitated river. The man in black was obviously tired. He reached the fast, dark brown water that slapped menacingly at the mudbanks. He paused for a moment, as if he thought that somehow he could turn back. Then in the fast-lightening gray of predawn he took his first step into the rapid shore current. The water was shallow, but he lost his footing and went down on one knee. Then he recovered and waded out another step.

Picard was only thirty feet away. Paulier glanced back and the detective saw his face as a ghoulish mask of white and black, drawn long by terror and fatigue. The fugitive's wading body jerked now as the bullets of the police pistols pounded into him. But he did not fall.

It was almost light. The devilish clown face stood out in detail. Suddenly that face tipped upward and the heavy lips parted in a sigh. The expression subtly transformed from terror and weariness to simple weariness. The man in black, now almost up to his waist, was still buffeted by the bullets, his body ticked by their impact, but still he did not fall.

Once more Paulier looked upward. The long face fixed on something in the direction of the city, but skyward. So searching was the gaze that Picard followed it. There he saw what Paulier scanned so deeply. There it was. The sun had limned a wispy line of summer clouds with new bright gold. It was the first full evidence of the day.

Still Paulier stared, questing in the gold clouds for something Picard could not imagine, oblivious to the shots and shouts of his pursuers. Then Paulier looked back to the water swirling around him and took a half-dozen more steps, swinging his body as he strode.

Sunlight, the first direct rays, fanned out from the east, and Picard saw the unbelievable. Paulier's body seemed to collapse within his garments, even as he moved into deeper water. The momentum of the river caught him at that instant and spun him into its deeps. Picard saw him once more as he was swept down: the eyes, neither dead nor fiery, were closed as if some last unseen friend had gently brushed them shut against the lighted world. With their fiery light hooded, the hideous face had almost the look of peace. The face, as it engraved itself on Picard's memory, was skull-like in fatigue—it was the face of one dead, thought Picard, who had seen so many.

CPSIA information can be obtained
at www.ICGtesting.com
Printed in the USA
JSHW050138130522
25811JS00001B/50

9 781954 321601